GEORGIAN PINEAPPLE SHUFFLE

TIME JUMPER

BOOK 2

HEIDE GOODY

IAIN GRANT

1

TIME JUMPER 2

It was the day before the stranger in the byre vanished, and a full five months before they would attempt to burn Alice Hickenhorn at the stake for her part in his disappearance.

"You look as if you could do with a posset," Granny Merrial said.

"Is that so?" said Alice Hickenhorn innocently. She knew this game and how it was played.

Merrial looked up from her seat by the wood fire but her fingers kept at her needlework. "Oh, yes, you do. There's a colour to your cheeks."

"What colour? Could it be the reddening of hot cheeks after a hard day's work."

"Oh, no," said Merrial. "'Tis a sallow colour, practically green. Are you sure your innards are not in flux?"

Alice turned to her. "My innards are exactly as they should be, granny."

"Don't be contradicting me," said Merrial. "You look ready to drop dead. You need a posset and..." She paused as though a thought had only just occurred to her. "I should have one too, just as a preventative, lest I catch what you clearly have."

"Is that so?"

Merrial nodded sagely. "Only thing to do. I shall make us both a posset. A nice reviving posset."

Alice brushed her hands on her smock. "Thank you, granny. I shall take my leisure then by the fire."

Merrial frowned. The old woman was more than a half century old and the frown lines in her face were deep things. "After you've milked the cow," she said.

"What?"

From her seat Merrial kicked the milk bucket in Alice's direction. "Can't make posset without milk. Get to it, lass."

"But surely, if I am so green that I look ready to drop, I should leave the milking to you."

"*Pfff,*" sneered Granny Merrial. "Hard work never killed no one."

To the unwitting observer, Granny Merrial might appear to be an old woman who could spot neither sarcasm in others nor hypocrisy in herself. But Alice was wise enough to know how well Merrial hid all manner of complex emotions and deceits behind a veil of apparent stupidity.

"Oh, then I'd best milk her," said Alice.

"Ah, might as well. You'll thank me for it later."

Alice picked up the bucket and headed out to the ramshackle byre where their one cow, Teasel, lived. It occurred to her, not for the first time, that Granny Merrial could simply say, "Go milk the cow, lass. I want to have a posset before my bed." But where was the fun in that, when the two of them could play their familiar game?

Teasel was a good cow as long as she was tended to promptly, first thing in the morning and before nightfall. The sun was setting over the town of Wirkswell, the buildings becoming deepening shadows, merging together until only the church spire and the many chimneys of the Swan Inn were distinctly visible from the mass of buildings.

Alice milked Teasel, singing to the girl all the while and giving her a loving pat when the bucket was full. Alice made a short tour of their plot before going back inside, tucking some of the herbs into her apron pocket so she could hang them up inside for drying. As she reached into her apron, she felt the comforting presence of her Polly Ann. Looking no more than a bumpy piece of wood, inexpertly carved by a mother Alice no longer remembered to vaguely resemble a girl, Polly Ann was a friend and treasured keepsake to Alice.

She looked up and saw a stranger approaching, coming down the track which led over the hill to the next town, Backnell. Alice had been to Backnell before, had even gone as far as Belper once. Some of the men in the town had been all the way to the city of Derby, but Alice wasn't sure if she'd enjoy going to foreign parts or like the food there.

The stranger was tall, unbent, and his clothes were fine. Pale hose were the choice of a city dweller. Alice knew of nobody who would wear such a thing when mud was a constant companion. His doublet was also unsullied. He smiled as he approached – but it was the smile of one who wished to present themselves as harmless. Alice could detect no warmth in it.

"I have need of lodgings," he said. He spoke in a manner she had never heard before: slowly and precise, with as little movement of his mouth as possible – as though he had a gold coin hidden in his mouth and didn't want to dislodge it.

"You'll want the Swan Inn, then. Down the road a way." She pointed towards the town.

"I would prefer to be here. You have a cowshed. I can make myself comfortable in there." He inclined a head towards Teasel's end of the building. There was a thick partition wall between the byre and living quarters, but all were housed inside the same building.

"I'll get Granny Merrial." Alice went inside as Merrial came out of the cottage and greeted the man.

"You are on business hereabouts?" Alice heard Merrial ask.

"Only for a few days," he replied. "I will be meeting with Master Burnleigh. If I could use your byre I would be most grateful." As Alice watched he pulled a coin from a bag and dropped it into Merrial's open hand.

"Very good," said Merrial. "I hope you're comfortable. What should we call you, sir?"

"You can call me Chamberlain."

Back in the kitchen, while Chamberlain made himself comfortable in the byre, Merrial went about her business of posset-making in the all-consuming way of an older person using a familiar space, clattering around in a purposeful way. She would use Teasel's milk, along with honey from the hives, as she did every day. The flavouring was where she might pause for inspiration. Herbs grew in every spare pocket of ground around their cottage, so she might choose rosemary if her gums were aching as they sometimes did. Alice hoped it wasn't a day for lavender, as Merrial used that when she was feeling faint – something which had been happening more often in recent months. The thought of Merrial becoming infirm was worrying.

"Lemon balm today, for clear thinking," Merrial declared.

Alice was all in favour of clear thinking, but she eyed Merrial, wondering what had prompted this.

The final and most important ingredient was a thimble-full of fortified wine added to each cup.

"We must be sure to take a plate round to Master Chamberlain when we eat," said Merrial.

"Yes," agreed Alice.

"Is there time to catch a rabbit? We should offer him meat."

"It's dark," said Alice.

Merrial made a disagreeable noise, as though it being night was the flimsiest of excuses.

"Do you want me to go and catch a rabbit?" Alice asked pointedly.

"No! I need you here in case he wants anything else. I am too old to run about."

"Well then, no rabbit. I am sure he will be happy with simple pottage," said Alice.

Merrial wasn't convinced. "I don't know. He must be a very fine gentleman. Did you see his hose?"

"I did see his hose. Very pale and fine. But tell me,

granny: if he has business with Master Burnleigh, then why would he not stay at the manor house, or at the inn?"

"Remember that we are simple women Alice. Do not question Master Chamberlain – not in his presence anyway. It strikes me that he wants to be somewhere out of the way, for his own reasons. Perhaps his business is of a delicate nature."

Alice was curious as to what that kind of business might be, but she would heed her granny's advice.

Merrial handed Alice the finished posset and, before they drank, offered her usual toast. "Let us have our wits but take care of how we share them."

Merrial insisted that while being a woman with knowledge was a good thing, it was better all round if the menfolk, especially those with book learning, remained unaware.

2

Later, when she took Master Chamberlain his pottage, Alice smiled politely but asked no questions. He had made a sleeping space for himself with some straw and had requested a bowl of water for washing. He travelled with very little luggage for a fine gentleman. If he had business papers then they must be hidden away in a pocket. Teasel looked across with mild curiosity, but kept to her own side of the byre.

"You know the town?" asked Chamberlain as he took the bowl.

"Yes, sir."

"What do you know of Master Burnleigh?"

"I know very little. We are but simple women, sir."

"So what little do you know? What is his reputation in these parts?"

Alice wondered what the correct answer might be.

Master Burnleigh owned the manor house and much of the land around. This was his town and he held sway.

"He has a reputation as a fair and just alderman. He attends the goose fair and makes buns available for the children."

"Buns, you say?"

"Aye." Alice felt sure that Chamberlain was fishing for something murky or scandalous. She lingered for a moment to see if he had any further questions, then left.

"What did he say to you?" Merrial asked, scraping out the last of her own bowl.

"He is curious about Master Burnleigh. Asking after his reputation. I told him that he provides buns for the children."

"A dull and middling answer, well done," said Merrial.

"I felt he wanted more."

"But you acted like a simple woman," nodded Merrial, satisfied.

"That I did."

In the morning, when Alice went to milk Teasel, she found Chamberlain was already up, and indicated that she must attend to the cow. He walked into town and was gone for many hours. He returned late in the afternoon, his expression not easy to read. Alice took him more pottage, but he did not speak to her.

"Well?" Merrial wanted to know what he'd said.

"If you have questions, you could visit him yourself," suggested Alice.

"Oh, what a whetstone it must have been to sharpen your tongue so, lass."

"He was entirely silent." Alice paused for a moment. "I thought I detected an air of frustration about him."

Merrial nodded, but neither of them had any further idea of what Chamberlain might be doing in the town.

"If he is anxious, perhaps we could administer a loosening draught?" Alice said. She avoided her granny's gaze.

"We most certainly will not!" Merrial said. "We are simple women, remember? We would do well to remember that women who administer herbs are not well-regarded by many gentlefolk. Especially as I suspect you want to loosen his tongue to satisfy your own curiosity."

Alice sighed. Merrial was right of course. Curiosity would be her undoing.

Alice was woken in the night by shouting.

"Merrial?" she whispered. "Someone is outside!"

"Aye." She heard Merrial's cot creak as she sat up.

"I'll take a look. I will be careful," said Alice. She made her voice brave, although she didn't feel brave.

She moved to the door and inched it open. She slipped out into the night, which was chilly but well-lit by the Moon. The noise was coming from the byre. One voice was Chamberlain, she was sure, and there was another, but she could not make out the words. Alice edged towards the door of the byre.

"Do not harm me!" shouted Chamberlain from inside.

Alice wondered what she might use as a weapon. Whether she intended to defend Chamberlain or herself, she wasn't certain, but she cast about for something. A pitchfork was wedged under the eaves, so she grabbed its handle. She stood for a moment, unsure whether to enter.

"Are you well, Master Chamberlain?" she called.

"Alice?" he replied, confused.

A blast of air knocked her off her feet. It was as if a great wind came from inside the byre, the roar of it loud in her ears. She stared, wondering what horror had made such a thing happen, but once the wind had subsided, all was quiet. There wasn't a single sound coming from within the byre, except for some ragged breaths from Teasel. She heard footsteps from behind.

"What has occurred?" said Merrial.

Alice turned to her and gave an exaggerated shrug to indicate she had no idea what was going on.

"Hello?" whispered Alice. She leaned in through the door. She saw Teasel scrabbling to her feet. Had the wind knocked her over? There was no sign at all of Master Chamberlain apart from his boots and his great cloak.

Alice stepped inside and put a calming hand on Teasel's head. "What happened Teasel?" she asked. "Where did they go?"

Nobody else was in the byre, that was clear. Alice turned to the doorway. Merrial stood there looking horrified and pasty pale.

"I don't understand," said Merrial. "There were two people in here. Nobody came past us."

Alice stooped to the straw where an indentation from Chamberlain's sleeping body remained. "It's still warm."

Merrial rushed in and grabbed Alice's face in her hands.

"Did you bring him a draught, Alice? Did you administer herbals?"

"No, I swear I did nothing!" Alice said.

Merrial looked very pale, and a sheen of sweat beaded her face.

"Are you feeling well, granny?"

"A calamity has befallen us, Alice. It is important that we remove all signs that anyone was here. We must greet the morning as if nothing at all has happened. I—" Merrial clutched her chest, breathing hard.

"Granny?"

Merrial managed to mouth a couple of words. She might have said 'Clear all signs' or something similar. But there was no sound from her lips. Merrial took a step, then her legs gave way and she slid to the floor.

3

It was a chill night when the townsfolk came to kill Alice, convinced by testimony of her magicking the man Chamberlain away and killing her own dear granny with devilish spells.

Alice was roughly handled from the front room of the Swan Inn, which had served as a court these last few days, and taken out into the street. She realised in horror that the pyre was already built. They had been so certain of the trial's outcome that everything was already in place.

She sought Master Burnleigh's face in the crowd. "Think upon your actions, Master Burnleigh, please!"

"Thou art a depraved and wicked girl, Alice Hickenhorn!" the church curate shouted in her face.

"I'm not," she said. "I am not! Neither depraved nor wicked!"

A street vendor, selling firewood from a wagon, was passing the last few remaining bundles to the outstretched hands which eagerly handed him coins. The man was literally selling wood that any fool could collect from the ground.

"Should you waste your pennies on such nonsense?" Alice spat at Mistress Green as the woman bought a bundle.

"That you should burn well!" said Mistress Green automatically, then had the decency to look embarrassed. "I thought they'd make a keepsake of the event."

"They're just sticks!"

"Commemorative sticks!" shouted the vendor. "Get them while you can!"

A man gave Alice a punch to the gut and she was dragged on to a small, raised platform which had been thoughtfully placed in the pyre for her to stand on so everyone could get a good look at her while she burned.

Children skipped in front of the wooden pile shouting excited nonsense.

"Burn the witch so we may have buns! Buns for the witch, buns for the witch!"

Was Master Burnleigh planning a celebration for afterwards? No wonder everyone was in high spirits. She saw no sorrow in people's faces, only excitement. No, that wasn't strictly true. As she stood with the stake rough against her shoulders, she could see some of the women looking on anxiously, as though they could see that what had happened to her might be possible for others.

Alice felt an uprising of anger. That she was going to die here was inevitable. How she met her death was the only thing left which she might control.

"Come on then! Bring on the flames! But know this. I am

no more a witch than any one of you. I go to my death knowing that I am guilty of no wrongdoing, which is more than can be said of you. You! Jack Harper, who I have oft seen poaching birds from the Burnleigh estate. And you Goody Marford, who has stolen many a garment from drying—"

"—Hurry! Set her alight!" came a rush of voices, panicked that Alice might share their secrets too.

Alice murmured a small prayer to her granny. "I am keeping my wits and taking care of how I share them, granny. It seems the least I can do." In her fist, she still clutched her little Polly Ann doll. That they would burn together was little consolation.

Torches were brought close and Alice could not help but stare at their bright yellow hearts.

It took her a few moments to realise there was a new sound among the hubbub of the idiot crowd, and that the townsfolk were no longer looking at her. Alice twisted as best she could and saw two figures come running down towards her. Her first thought was that they were the strangest fey creatures she had ever seen. Their hands were bright points of sparkling fire, as though each of them held an actual star in their grasp. And it was hard to ascertain if their clothing clung unnaturally close to their female bodies, or if their very hides were flappy folds of dark leather and fabric.

One of the creatures yelled, a wordless roar. The other swung its arms about and bellowed, "I am the god of hellfire!"

Alice should have been terrified, but she seemed to have expended all her terror in preparing to be burned alive. By comparison, these magical beings were a jolly and welcome distraction.

"Demons!" spluttered Master Harper in fear.

The townsfolk cowered as the creatures ran at them. Mistress Green even threw her commemorative sticks at one to try to ward it off.

"Fire! To destroy all you've done!" shouted one demon. A great ball of flame shot from her hand and flew straight at Master Burnleigh and the other aldermen.

Alice didn't even notice that the other demon had untied her hands and as the magic ball of flame exploded with a crack as loud as thunder, the demon took her by the hand and hauled her away.

Alice did not resist or argue. Demons or not, running away was a good thing. She willingly followed them into the darkness and up the hill.

IT TOOK Alice quite some time to put the pieces of a most disturbing day into place and accept that the demons – Astrid and Maddie – were not demons at all, but everyday woman. Albeit women from an inconceivable future time.

Beer helped make Alice accept this new situation. They sat in a futuristic drinking house, as large and as clean as any church. The beer put in front of Alice was foamy and effervescent, and had a taste far softer than any beer she had drunk before, yet it was stronger.

The one called Astrid did not drink beer but a bubbling

clear liquid called a gin and tonic which, for some reason, had a piece of exotic fruit floating in it.

This world was powerful strange and Alice decided there would be some things she would like about it and others she would not. "So, this is over four hundred years after my own time?" she asked.

"That's right," said the one called Maddie.

"But I'm not all maggots and dust."

"Seemingly not."

Alice sipped beer as she digested this thought. Eventually, she asked. "Do I have to go back to my own time?"

"Don't you want to go back to your own time?" said Astrid.

Alice thought about the scenes of hatred which had surrounded her in her final moments in Wirkswell town square and laughed bitterly. "Not likely, madam. You saw how shoddily treated I was. Nothing I want from there except my cow and—" She gasped and patted the wide pocket in the front of her dress. "Polly Ann!"

"We left it on Astrid's desk," said Maddie. "Sorry."

Astrid produced Alice's dolly from the strange bag she carried and Alice snatched it up will glee.

"Important to you?" said Maddie.

"My best friend, save the bees and my cow," said Alice, realising they had indeed left Teasel behind.

"That's so sad," said Maddie.

"Tragic," said Astrid. "I suppose you can stay at mine. On the sofa, mind."

"So-fa," said Alice. The word meant nothing.

"I have a spare bedroom, although I am putting you in a shower first."

"Shower?" said Alice.

By the next day, Alice had concluded that sofas belonged in the list of things she would like in this new world. Showers, however, belonged in the list of things she would not.

4

The following morning, Maddie Waites lay in bed and stared at the ceiling. It was Saturday, a day off from her job in the Amenities and Facilities office at Wirkswell town hall. She needed time to just lie still and think. It had been a weird old twenty-four hours. Well, no, it hadn't been twenty-four hours at all. Due to weird looping skips in time that saw her reliving Friday at least three times in a row, the last twenty-four hours had lasted several days.

And yet, across all the madness she had endured, one moment stuck with her: the conversation she'd had with the singer of another band not long after she'd returned from her jaunt to rescue Alice from Ye Olde Englande times.

"You're talking about Skid, right?" she'd asked.

"A dear friend," the singer had replied.

"Yeah. Sorry about earlier. Um, when did he die?"

"Last Wednesday."

"Like the most recent Wednesday or...?"

"*The Wednesday of last*

"*Right, right. And the road*

"*Why?*"

"*Please.*"

"*The Baslow Road. Up by the Shell gar*

"*Ah. I know the spot.*"

All that travel and opportunity, and now he

on the possibility that they could save the life of

motorcyclist. The challenge. *Could* they save the life

young motorcyclist?

Maddie shook her head. They'd only just discovered time

travel. They didn't want to get ahead of themselves. Best seek

another hour's sleep, recoup some energy and—

"Are you putting the kettle on or not?" shouted Uncle

Kevin from downstairs.

Maddie groaned. The man might have mobility

problems. He might need help around the house. But

his converted downstairs bedroom was a dozen steps

from the kitchen. The man could put on a kettle

himself.

"Yes, Kevin!" she called.

The lie-in was over. She threw her quilt back, walked

barefoot to the bathroom to pee and mutter tired obscenities

to herself as she sat there to think.

Around her wrist was the woven woollen friendship

bracelet Gregory had given her, the inexplicable source of

her time-travelling abilities. She hadn't really worked out

how the thing functioned yet. Mostly, the jumps in time had

occurred at moments of stress, of blind panic. She, or one of

the other people holding onto her, would urgently need to be week."

e died on?"

ge."

r mind fixated

one young

of one

19

ckwards in

he raggedy
phone. She
t, please."

tired fury

ning of the
t seat being
oked at her
tomatically
half hours

She went to flush the toilet, but now, three hours earlier, there was nothing there to flush. She washed her hands and went out onto the dark landing. She couldn't go back to her own bed: her earlier sleeping self was already there, and she didn't want to either wake herself or have to spoon herself in that single bed.

The other bedroom upstairs had once been Aunt Cathy and Uncle Kevin's. It had been unoccupied for several years, but the double bed and mattress were still there. Maddie silently took pillows and a musty unaired blanket from the wardrobe and made herself comfortable. It was not the best bed, but three and a bit hours of extra sleep time were not to be sniffed ~~out.~~ at.

And she did sleep, to be woken later by the sound of Kevin shouting, "Are you putting the kettle on or not?" and her own earlier reply of "Yes, Kevin!"

Maddie rose and went to the bathroom. She waited for the sound of her quiet angry hiss of "Oh, come on! Please!" before going in. The bathroom was empty. Maddie flushed the toilet for her earlier self and began her morning ablutions for real.

An hour later, she was banging on Astrid Bohart's front door. She'd tried ringing the doorbell but had got no response. "Astrid! Alice!"

Maddie was there for a good five minutes, and couldn't understand why she was being ignored. Astrid's suburban semi-detached had cameras at several points on the outside wall, and Astrid herself had some serious security paranoia, so Maddie was fairly certain she hadn't been overlooked.

What was starting to concern her was the distant screaming. Should she break in?

The door was flung open with an earthy grunt and Astrid stood there in a zipped up Hi-Viz workman's raincoat. The middle-aged woman's face was red with effort, or frustration. Her waterproof was wet and her trousers were soaked through.

"Everything OK?" Maddie asked. "I heard some noises."

"Alice and I were having a small disagreement on matters of personal hygiene," said Astrid.

"She been trying to kill me!" Alice appeared, wearing a hooded dressing gown. "Made me wet all over and pulled my hair out."

Alice Hickenhorn did sort of look like what Maddie had expected an olden times woman to look like. She had been dirty, her clothes rags, and her hair had been a wild thicket of knots. Send her back in time a couple of decades, dye it black, and her crazy back-combed hair would have made a fine goth. But, for now, it just looked like the kind of mass in which a bird might make its home. Or possibly a small family of badgers.

Maddie sighed sympathetically. "Ah. You'll have some wicked tangles in there I expect."

"Indeed," said Astrid, drawing herself up haughtily and shaking off some of the water. "I did say it's a case of putting up with some short-term pain, or we simply cut it all off and start afresh."

Maddie stepped inside. "You know how you said you didn't want to go back to your own time Alice? Well, we have to do some work so that you fit in here. I'll take a look at your hair."

Alice reflexively held out a hand. "Don't you be hurting me an' all."

"Another pair of eyes on the problem can't hurt," said Maddie. "I won't do anything unless you tell me I can." She suspected Astrid had a lot less patience than she did.

"Good luck to you, I say," snorted Astrid.

Maddie tilted her head. "Let's have a drink. We'll have a gentle look at Alice's hair, then we're going to discuss how we're going to save Skid."

"We're doing what?" said Astrid.

5

S oon enough, they were all sipping tea in Astrid's living room (although Astrid noticed that the ungrateful time-traveller Alice was pulling a face at the taste).

Alice sat in the armchair beneath Astrid's sagging shelves of research books while Maddie did some far too gentle namby-pamby de-tangling of Alice's hair with a wide-toothed comb. "You know what might help here? If I comb through some conditioner to make your hair slippery, then we can rinse it out afterwards. We might do well to trim the split ends while we're at it."

"How often do you folks do this thing of getting wet all over?" said Alice.

"Every day," said Maddie. "Most people anyway."

"Even your hair?" Alice said in horror. "Makes the chill take a proper hold that does. Can kill a person."

"Hair can be every other day," said Maddie.

"We have heated homes and hairdryers, so it's not a cause of death these days," said Astrid, waggling the hairdryer on the armrest of her chair.

"What's that?" said Alice.

"Hairdryer. Hair. Dryer." Astrid repeated the name slowly. It seemed the young woman needed things repeating. Astrid reached down to the plug, switched it on, and directed a blast at Alice.

"Oh!" She seemed equally delighted and dismayed. "Warm air where I want it? This time is truly blessed." Alice blew air onto her arms and legs. She refused to switch it off, which meant they all had to raise their voices to talk over it.

"Why do we want to save this Skid character then?" said Astrid loudly.

"It seems a natural thing to do," Maddie replied, equally loudly.

"Did you know him?"

"No."

"Then why?"

"Do I have to know someone in order to save them?"

"Not at all," said Astrid. "Although there is a surplus of people in the world at the moment. It's not like we're running out."

"You're saying you don't want to save his life?"

"You want reasons?"

"I want reasons."

Astrid held up a hand and ticked off her fingers. "One: you don't know him, at all. Two: he is already dead. He's not getting any deader. He's not suffering. Three: it's a fixed point in time. It has happened and the world has moved on. The world does not care if he's alive or dead. Four: he killed himself in a silly motorbike crash. He was responsible for his own death. And five – which is a big one – he's called Skid. I mean, really, Maddie. He's called Skid. Does that sound like the name of a person worth saving?"

Maddie stared at her. Glaring at Astrid was not the correct response, since the woman had logically taken down Maddie's foolish notion.

Alice was blasting the hairdryer directly into her own face. "This is wonderful!" she said, grinning.

"Reasons to save him," said Maddie, raising her own fingers. "One: any life is worth saving. He's just gonna be the first. Two: he had a family. He had parents."

"Did he?" said Astrid.

"I dunno. Probably. And they're suffering now. They're experiencing a loss. Three: we don't know if he was responsible for his own death. We weren't there. Four: his name doesn't matter, does it? And, um, five—" Maddie frowned. "Five: this would be an ideal way of testing the practicalities of time travel. Like, in an experiment."

Astrid reached over, snatched the hair dryer off Alice, and turned the annoying thing off. "What do you mean?"

Maddie spread her hands. "We've used the time travel bracelet four or five times. I don't think we've ever used it willingly or with a solid idea of where we intended to travel."

"When," said Alice.

"This—" continued Maddie "—this would be an opportunity for us to use the time bracelet to do a single, focussed jump back in time, make a specific change to history, and return to the present day."

"We're going to step back through time again?" said Alice.

"Only to last Wednesday. The guy at the bar said it was on the Baslow Road, up by the Shell garage."

Astrid had to admit she was intrigued by the notion. They had barely tapped the potential of the time travelling friendship bracelet. She was going to suggest they could use it to explore the past, gather research and, yes, maybe find some evidence for certain personal theories she'd been arguing about on the Twittersphere and with the Facebook mob. "A test run."

"Exactly," said Maddie.

"And if we do go back to last Wednesday, how do we stop foolish Mr Skid from killing himself? Do you think he will drive more slowly if we ask him?"

"We would need to put the fear of God in him," said Alice.

Maddie hummed thoughtfully. Astrid realised she was looking at her – specifically at her Hi-Viz waterproof and the hair dryer in her hand.

"Have you got a pair of smart dark trousers?" said Maddie.

"What of it?" said Astrid.

"And maybe another one of those luminous jackets?"

ON REFLECTION, Astrid was forced to agree it was an intriguing plan.

The three of them walked through the town, over the river and towards the Baslow Road. Alice had wanted to put her old clothes on, but Astrid explained they were still in the washing machine and would not be clean or dry for another couple of hours. Privately, Astrid hoped they would be ripped apart in the wash so that the fetid rags could be tossed into a bin. Astrid had subsequently dressed the girl in some simple trousers and a hoodie. The hood would at least hide Alice's still tangled thatch of hair.

Astrid herself had put on her interview trousers and found a second hi-vis jacket for Maddie to wear.

Alice gazed about herself as they walked, drinking in the sights and sounds of the twenty-first century. Astrid thought she'd taken the concept of cars and other road vehicles in her stride, even if Maddie's explanation of how they worked had been somewhat lacking.

"So, they have little stoves inside, and the stove's heat excites the wheels to turn?" said Alice, nodding.

"Yes," said Maddie. "Sort of."

"And the Shell garage is a place where they get the fuel for their contraptions."

"Yes. Petrol. It's a sort of oil."

"I know what oil is. And so we jump back to Wednesday and wait all day for a man on his two-wheel contraption to come along?"

"I don't think we'll have to wait that long," said Maddie.

Astrid and Alice waited on the petrol station forecourt while Maddie went inside. She was not long. She came out with a smile on her face and a Snickers in her hand. Astrid stared at the chocolate bar.

"You bought something?"

"I had to look like a proper customer," said Maddie. "The guy was very helpful. It happened around lunchtime."

Astrid nodded. She had had her reservations about this plan, mostly because it wasn't her plan, but she was warming to it. She held up the hairdryer in her hand. She'd fed the plug and lead up her sleeve so that the L-shaped dryer was the only thing poking out.

"Let's play at being cops," said Maddie.

6

Alice had been too bewildered and frightened to properly recall her first jaunt through time, but now had the luxury of observing one in the cool, bright light of day. Maddie led them behind a stone wall just down from the Shell garage.

"Right. I think we all need to hold hands," she said.

"We're not friends," said Astrid. "You know that, right?"

"I mean, I am the one with the bracelet—"

"Yes, about that. I do think that we ought to discuss giving it to someone with a bit more—"

"*I* am the one with the bracelet," Maddie repeated forcefully, "so you will need to be in physical contact with me. I think it works by me focussing my intentions."

"Oh, it's a magic wishing bracelet," said Alice.

"We are never calling it that," said Astrid.

"Is it not magic?"

Maddie saw the tight uncomfortable look on Astrid's face. "I'm not sure Astrid or I believe in magic, Alice."

"I deny all spiritual things," said Astrid firmly.

"So it works through natural philosophies," said Alice. "Like the cars?"

"We don't know how it works," said Maddie.

"But you make a wish in your head and it takes you there? It sounds very much like a magic wishing bracelet."

"All I do," said Maddie, taking out the device which Alice now knew was a 'phone', "is I look at the time and date, and I think to myself what the phone would look like at the time and date where I want to go to and—" The sky was suddenly cloudy, the air instantly a mite warmer. Maddie consulted her phone. "—and we're here."

"Wait," said Astrid. "Have you done this before?"

"I may have had a tiny practice run this morning," said Maddie, then looked at her phone. The numbers on it flickered and changed. "I *will* have a tiny practice run next Saturday morning." She smiled sweetly, like a child who had stolen an apple.

Astrid gave an annoyed humph and made her way out onto the road. Alice and Maddie followed.

"And now the plan is for you and Astrid to stand at the side of the road and pretend to be constables of the parish. You will aim your special pistol—"

"We're pretending it's a speed gun," said Maddie.

The words meant nothing to Alice. "—And this Skid will be so afeared of the speed gun that he will slow down."

"Basically. Yes."

"Can I not also pretend to be a constable of the parish?"

"We've only got the two coats."

"You can give me yours."

"Your hair is still a mess," said Astrid. "You look like a tramp."

"Not cool," said Maddie.

"I can't call her a tramp?"

"Not in that sense. Not in any sense. A homeless person is a homeless person, or a person struggling with homelessness."

"You're saying I look like a vagrant?" said Alice.

"Indeed," said Astrid. "A vagrant. A vagabond."

"I feel insulted," said Alice and crossed her arms fiercely.

"If you'd let us fix your hair you wouldn't be."

Maddie held out the wrapped object she had purchased from the Shell garage. "Snickers?"

"Snickers to you too, madam!" Alice retorted.

Maddie rolled her eyes. "It's chocolate. Food. You'll like it."

Alice took it begrudgingly and sat a distance from Maddie and Astrid while they took their position on the bend of the road, Astrid holding out the hairdryer as though it was the speed pistol which supposedly put the fear of God into the car drivers. Indeed, it seemed to be working. Many of the drivers did slow their vehicles sharply at the sight of them.

Alice unwrapped the food bar and, initially put off by the brown earthy colour of the item, nibbled at its corner carefully. It was extremely sweet, as sweet as honey and its flavours were alien to her but – by all that was holy! – she did indeed like it.

A short time later a motorcyclist on a black bike slowed and tucked in behind a car he was about to overtake. Less than a heartbeat later, a vast vehicle – a 'lorry' – came past in the other direction.

Astrid and Maddie gave confirming nods to one another and walked over to Alice.

"And is that it?" said Alice. "Master Skid is saved from death."

"Apparently so," grinned Maddie.

"I expected something more dramatic."

"There was no drama. That was sort of the point. Our job is done."

"It was a successful experiment," Astrid agreed reluctantly. "Now, let us discuss putting it to proper use, and also who should be custodian of this great power."

"I'm not giving you the friendship bracelet," said Maddie. "It's mine. It's got my name on it."

"It says 'Mad'," said Astrid.

"Gregory only had a few letters available."

"Who is Gregory?" said Alice.

"One of Maddie's reprobate friends," said Astrid.

"He's not a reprobate," said Maddie.

"He trespasses onto the old allotments to grow weed in the abandoned greenhouses."

"Yes," Maddie admitted. "Okay, he does do that. But that doesn't make him a reprobate."

"He stole the wool to make that bracelet from the Burnley Manor compost bins."

"Magic wool?" said Alice.

"It's not—" Maddie took a breath. "It might be very special wool."

Astrid frowned at her. "Magic wool?"

"Obviously, there's no such thing as magic wool but—"

"If we could fashion more bracelets..."

"If it is the wool—"

"To the allotments!" Astrid declared, and before anyone could disagree marched off towards town and the allotments up on the hill.

7

M addie led the way into the allotments through a crack in the metal fence.

"So, this land is for the local people to grow their own food?" said Alice, noting the abandoned plots around the place.

"Very much that," said Astrid.

"But it is barren."

"Council closed the allotments."

"Probably going to sell the land off," added Maddie.

"And the people will starve?" said Alice.

"Nah. They'll just go get their food from the supermarket."

"Super market," mused Alice. "How super?"

"Er, fairly super."

"We had the Goose Fair come round each August. That was quite super."

"Yes, our supermarket is a different kind of super," said Maddie. "We'll show you later. Through here..."

She led the way through a gap in the hedges and into the fruitless orchard beyond. The other two followed.

"I recognise this place," said Alice. "The hill. The curve of the land..." She pointed at the big old house which could be seen at some distance. "Master Burnleigh's house stood there."

"Burnley Manor," nodded Astrid.

"Master Burnleigh's house was not so grand," said Alice.

Astrid sniffed and gave the high stone house some consideration. "Looks Georgian by my reckoning. Built at least a hundred years after your time."

Alice chuckled. "My time? Don't reckon I have a time anymore."

Maddie led on to the shed and the compost bin composed of pallets leaning against its side. "Here." She did not have to dig deep into the surface before coming up with ripped fragments of knitted wool. "This is the stuff Gregory re-wove into the friendship bracelet."

"It sounds like a special friendship you two have," said Alice.

Maddie totally caught her tone. "God, no. Nothing like that. We're not ... betrothed or anything. I'm not sure if I'm even into men."

Astrid pulled back, surprised. "You're a lesbian?"

"I don't have to answer that question."

"Is it a difficult question?"

"Are you putting a label on me?"

"You were the one who raised it."

"I was just..." Maddie growled. "I was just saying Gregory and I don't have a thing going on. Friendship bracelets aren't like that."

"No," Astrid agreed. "Friendship bracelets are things that nine-year-old girls give each other."

"And good adult platonic friends. Come on, let's bag this stuff up and weave some more friendship bracelets back at yours, Astrid."

"Bracelets. Not friendship bracelets," said Astrid.

"What's the difference?"

"We're not friends."

"Ouch."

Astrid scoffed. "It's nothing to be offended about. I have known you barely more than a day. I can't promote you to the rank of 'friend' just like that."

"Promote, huh?"

Astrid nodded. "Friend is very specific descriptor. I have to take a lot of things into consideration before making that commitment."

"We can be friends. Making friends is easy. Alice's best friends are a cow and a wooden doll."

"They are," Alice agreed cheerfully.

"And you think this gives credence to your point of view?" said Astrid. "If Alice tells you you're her friend, you know you have been placed on the same level as farm animals and lumps of wood. Now, if you should ever be regarded as my friend, well..." Astrid made a sighing noise as though mightily impressed. "That's a rare and sought after honour."

"Uh-huh." Maddie stuffed the clumps of wool into her jacket pocket. "So who is your best friend?"

"The criteria is strict."

"Yeah? So...?"

"The position is vacant at the moment," Astrid said stiffly. "Have we got all the wool?"

"I've got enough," Maddie said, wiping her hands on the hi-vis to get rid of the worst of the muck.

"You'll clean that off my coat when we get home," said Astrid.

"No problem, friend-o," Maddie smiled.

They pushed back through the hedge and into the allotments. There was a loud and startled shout of "Fuck!" and in front of them, on the ground, was Gregory – fallen over in literal surprise at seeing them. He blinked hard. "Maddie?"

"Hi Gregory," said Maddie.

"Fuck. I thought you were the filth."

Maddie could see Alice's confusion. "He thinks we're constables of the parish."

Astrid pointed the hairdryer at him. "Thought this was a raid, druggy?"

Gregory stumbled to his feet and pushed his flopping curly hair away from his face.

"He's tall, isn't he?" said Alice.

"Men are giants in this time," said Maddie.

Gregory flicked a finger at Alice and Astrid. "Sorry. Who are these people?"

"Alice. Astrid," said Maddie. "Remember. You met them at the Old Schoolhouse last night."

"Schoolhouse?"

"The gig."

His dark eyebrows descended in a frown. "We haven't played a gig at the Old Schoolhouse since..."

Astrid gripped Maddie's arm and murmured, "Today is Wednesday."

"Crap," said Maddie. How could she travel back in time and somehow forget? "I *mean* that these are my friends, Alice and Astrid—"

"Not a friend," put in Astrid.

"—and that I *am going to* invite them to the gig at the Old Schoolhouse next Friday."

"I see. Good. You had a problem with your tenses there. What were you doing back there?"

"Just having a poke around," said Maddie. "Seeing what we might find."

"Find anything good?" said Gregory.

She couldn't tell him about the wool, could she? How could she? He'd told her about the wool. He couldn't tell her and then she tell him. That was one of them circular paradox things, wasn't it? "Oh, this and that. Probably worth exploring yourself sometime."

He smiled. "Okay. Maybe I will."

"She's a lesbian," said Astrid. "Just in case you get any ideas."

Maddie gave Astrid a look of such intense disgust she felt her eyeballs wanting to vomit. "I am not—" she began, paused, tried to take a breath, and started again. "I am not fond of labels."

"It's all cool," shrugged Gregory. "You know I'm happy with whatever."

Maddie tried to smile at him, but her emotions wouldn't let her. She grabbed Astrid by the elbow and hauled her to the exit, Alice following close behind.

"You are such an embarrassment!" Maddie hissed.

"I don't think you're a lesbian," said Astrid coolly.

MADDIE TRIED to find her calm centre as they walked back into town.

"We should talk about our plans for making good use of this interesting opportunity we've been given," said Astrid, oblivious to the hurt and annoyance she had caused.

"Maybe go back in time and slap the stupids out of you before you put your foot in it," suggested Maddie.

"What's a lesbian?" said Alice.

"Google it," said Maddie.

"You do have funny words in this new age."

"We need to prioritise some of our most basic needs," Astrid went on.

"What?" said Maddie.

"What do we need to use time travel for?"

"To get an extra few hours of sleep seems a good goal," said Maddie.

Astrid considered this. "You're familiar with Maslow's hierarchy of needs, of course?"

"Maslow," said Alice. "He's the one as sings them dirty

songs. Comes round with the Goose Fair. I likes the one about the Prick of the Hedgehog."

Maddie and Astrid stared at her.

"I quite want to hear that song," Maddie admitted.

"No," said Astrid firmly. "The Maslow *I'm* thinking of created a structure which helps us consider what a person needs in order to achieve great things. It is not possible unless certain basic needs are met. We need food, shelter, safety and so on."

"Enough time," said Maddie. "Kip. Shut eye. Like I said."

"Well yes," said Astrid. "So far, so obvious. What I really mean to say is that we have the means to satisfy our most basic needs, thus freeing ourselves to concentrate on the business of doing amazing things."

"I have a feeling Astrid is suggesting that we secure ourselves some money to support our efforts," said Maddie.

"Exactly that! If Alice plans to stop here, I can see my energy bills about to go up, although she might want to think about getting herself a job," said Astrid.

"A job?" said Alice. "I've never had a job before."

"Was witching not a full-time job?" said Maddie.

"I'm not a witch."

"Or maybe Alice does not need to get a job if we can make money from time travel."

"How does that work?" said Maddie. "Give time tours to millionaires?"

Astrid became animated. "It should be as simple as this. We know that everyday things from the past are valuable now, right? Well, all we have to do is go back and hide a few things in a safe place, then we can go and get them. Bingo! Antiques we can sell for a tidy sum."

"Old things are valuable?" said Alice. "Are not new things worth more?"

"Antique items accrue value because of their rarity."

"Ah, 'tis because of lost skills. Reverend Buttle says we are but dwarfs standing on the shoulders of giants."

"It's none of that nonsense," said Astrid. "I would have thought one day in this place would have shown you that we live in a golden age. Trust me. Antiques are worth money. We go back in time, hide them—"

"Not just bring them back with us?" said Maddie.

"Then they wouldn't be old, numbskull."

"All right, lady. So, where would be a safe place? People poke around in every place you can think of, surely? Especially when they have centuries to do it."

"Ah. Aha! Well that is the really clever part! We go and look around the graveyard, find a really old grave and jump to somewhere after that person was buried. We stash the goodies inside the grave, where they should stay undisturbed until we go and dig them out." Astrid grinned at her own genius.

Alice looked bemused at the idea.

Maddie wasn't sure where to start. "So we have to mess with someone's grave. Twice."

Astrid waved a dismissive hand. "Should be straightforward enough."

"And how do we get hold of the things which we plan to stash? We don't have any olde worlde money or anything."

"We can trade things that will be valued," said Astrid.

"Like the hairdryer?" said Alice, pointing at the one in Astrid's hand.

"It wouldn't work if we went back any length of time," said Maddie. "There's a whole load of modern things that wouldn't work. What were you thinking, Astrid?"

"I'll show you," said Astrid with a wink. "Let's get Alice decent and we'll all take a trip into town."

8

They walked past the shops of Wirkswell, Alice staring at the goods for sale. There were several businesses that Astrid knew they would struggle to explain. Something about having a wide-eyed and naïve ingénue by her side swelled Astrid's chest with pleasure. To have someone to guide and to mould, a young person who was not yet jaded by the modern world... It was like being a teacher again, and not a teacher of bottom set year nine boys, but a teacher of keen and eager year sevens.

"Nail bar," she said. "That is not for today. Add it to the list of things we will talk about later. Same with vaping."

"I know vaping," said Alice. "'Tis the inhaling of pleasurable relaxants."

"Huh." Astrid couldn't help being impressed with the speed of learning and general adaptability Alice seemed to have. Best to get all her teaching in before Alice learned it all herself.

A shop that drew Alice's attention as much as any was a simple old-fashioned greengrocers. The bright colours of the fruit and vegetables on display seemed to captivate her.

"These are all real?" she said. She picked up a mango and sniffed it.

"Mango," said Maddie. "Don't suppose you had those in your time."

Alice stroked an avocado. "'Tis hard and bumpy."

"The fruit is soft and green."

"And far too popular with the young middle classes," said Astrid.

Alice grabbed at a pineapple and recoiled with a yelp at its hard pointy surface.

"Come along," said Astrid, pulling Maddie to the next shop. "This is the place I wanted us to explore. We can equip Alice with the basics she'll need, and also get some things which will have a high value in the past."

"The Gertrude Foundation charity shop?" said Maddie. "Yeah. Good shout. What sort of thing should we take back, though?"

"Small things like gloves, belts and hats could work well I reckon," said Astrid as she pushed open the door.

"Such beautiful things!" said Alice, twirling in the centre of the shop, entranced.

Astrid saw the two assistants glance at each other. She guessed most customers did not react with such enthusiasm. "These things are especially good," she said, steering Alice towards the fifty pence rail.

Maddie rolled her eyes at Astrid and opened her purse.

"Come on, we need her to dress like a regular person. What kind of budget can we rustle up?"

Between the two of them they agreed a modest budget for Alice's clothes, and a selection of tradable goods which might appeal to people from the pre-industrial era.

"I do wonder if this is the most straightforward plan," said Maddie. "There are quite a lot of things that could go wrong. Surely there is a simpler way to get some money?"

"Oh yes? Like what?" Astrid stared at Maddie, mainly to avoid the sight of Alice parading round in a huge fluffy jumper in lime green.

"Well, what if we went back and got a famous pop star to scribble some of their songs on a napkin? That would be simple to bring back and should be really valuable."

"A pop star? Really?" Astrid sighed. "Well it is simple, I'll give you that."

"Thank you."

Astrid hadn't meant it as a compliment. "Fine. Why don't we do both things? We can see what works best."

Maddie nodded in agreement.

Alice had been trying things on the whole time. Astrid had assumed she was entirely distracted, but apparently not.

"Adventures in the past are all well and good, but won't you pair still look like demons to the eyes of folk like me?" Alice indicated their outfits. "I'll be fine cos I still have my things." She caught a look on Astrid's face and her eyes narrowed. "I do still have my things, don't I?"

Astrid rolled her eyes. "They might have survived a trip through the washing machine."

Alice spotted something and lunged across the shop.

"Something like this is what you need." She held up a hanger.

Maddie read the tag. "It's a pair of curtain linings." She looked up at Astrid and with a shrug added it to the growing pile at the counter.

Alice had selected several dresses, skirts and tops, but took some convincing to try on any trousers.

"Try these, they are stretchy and comfortable," said Maddie and passed her a pair of leggings.

Alice disappeared into the changing cubicle and came out making exaggerated lunging motions. "So much movement is possible!"

Maddie nodded in encouragement. "Yep. Let's add it to the pile."

Maddie turned to Astrid. "So if we do my plan? If we go back to something like the early seventies and meet George Michael or David Bowie or the Beatles—"

"You have a weak grasp of what music happened when, Maddie Waites."

"But do you know what people used to wear then?"

"Are you asking me because I'm a historian or because I'm old?" Astrid asked.

"The history thing, obviously," said Maddie, but she took a fraction too long to think about it.

9

Maddie could see that Alice was delighted with her haul of charity shop clothes. She chattered endlessly about the colours and styles as they walked away down the high street.

"What I don't understand is how you can manage your courses while wearing these tight-fitting things," she said, practising more of her crazy lunges. Alice had refused to remove the jogging bottoms.

"Ah," said Maddie. "By courses you mean monthly bleeding? Your period?"

Alice nodded.

"How did you manage bef—?" Maddie stopped herself. "Tell you what, it doesn't matter. Let's get you some gear from the twenty first century and hopefully that will explain things. We'll pop in here."

They went into the chemist and grabbed a basket.

Astrid moved in front of Maddie and held up a hand. "Wait, we've already spent enough money on Little Miss Time Traveller."

Maddie rolled her eyes. "We're going to get some money soon, remember? We can't leave Alice with no means of managing her period. She will need a few other personal items too. Like a hairbrush."

As they went round the shop, they piled in what felt like the bare essentials.

"These things here," said Alice, holding up a packet, "with a picture of toes. What is this?"

"Um. That there is a piece of shaped rubber to separate your toes so you don't make a mess when you paint your toenails."

Alice looked at Maddie, at the pink rubber item in its packet again, then at Astrid. "Painting toenails. We do this for frolics, at festivals and times of dancing, yes?"

"Yes." Maddie was relieved Alice had grasped the frivolous nature of the idea immediately. "That is what quite a lot of the stuff in here is for. Painting our faces, making ourselves look nice. Plenty of it is nonsense, mind. We'll build up your knowledge of that as we go." Maddie thought for a moment. "Tell you what, we could get you a magazine to flick through."

"Over my dead body!" Astrid declared. "Unrealistic beauty ideals and terrible role models. Beauty magazines have a lot to answer for."

"What is a magazine? It sounds exciting!" said Alice.

They ended up with another large bag of purchases from the chemist.

"Now to find a suitable grave," said Astrid.

Maddie wasn't wild about the idea of traipsing around graveyards. "Only one of us needs to do that, surely?"

"It is imperative that we all have a good knowledge of its location, so we can use it to drop off our treasures," said Astrid.

"It's just that I need to get back to Kevin."

"Who is Kevin?" said Alice.

"My uncle. I live in his house and care for him. My aunt died a few years back and he's got mobility problems."

"His problems move around?"

"No, I mean he has, er, disability."

Alice seemed none the wiser.

"He's a cripple," said Astrid.

"Astrid!"

"She understood the reference!" Astrid protested, pointing to Alice's comprehending face.

"That's not the point!" said Maddie. "You are not using this situation to use words we stopped using for a good reason. Anyhow, I need to get back to Kevin at some point. Our neighbour will watch him for a while, but I can't push my luck."

"You don't need to get back to Kevin until next Saturday," said Astrid. "Right now, past Maddie is looking after him."

"Fine, but when we get back to Saturday, I don't want to leave him too long."

"Then you jump back to moments after you left. You can spend more quality time with him."

"What? Is this my life now? I have to have two of me every

day so that I can do the things I need to do and the things I want to do?"

Astrid and Alice exchanged a look that suggested it was exactly the case.

"But..." Maddie struggled to articulate why this made her uneasy. "What will that mean – if I keep doing it? Will the working Maddie come to resent the Maddie that gets to go off and play?"

"There is only one Maddie," said Alice. "You just get two goes at each day."

"Fine."

"Admittedly, in real time, you will be aging far faster than the rest of us."

"What?"

"Not a bad thing," suggested Astrid. "I think there were decades in the past that I'd happily live in for twenty years."

Alice pulled a packet of sanitary towels from their shopping bag. "Now can I open these to see?"

Maddie nodded.

Alice pulled at the packet and removed a pad. She put it to her face and felt its softness against her cheek. "So very soft, and so very white! 'Tis strange to make them white. Rags are always better if they are dark coloured. Who decided to make them white?"

Maddie hesitated. She had never considered that question. It *was* weird.

"Men," said Astrid with a weary sigh. "No women were consulted back in the day. Men decided in their wisdom that sanitary products must look like surgical dressings."

Maddie had no idea if that was correct, but it sounded plausible.

They walked back to Astrid's house with Alice continuing to cosset the sanitary towel as if it was a cute little pet.

10

Alice recognised the church from her own time. "A building was here, yes, but not this one. Not exactly."

Astrid rubbed her hands with satisfaction. "Superb. Well, it's obvious many of the additions we see here are from Victorian times. Perhaps Alice remembers a smaller building that would correspond to the central nave area?"

"Aye," said Alice. She had learned that Astrid was at her best once she had made her point and everyone agreed with her. She pointed. "Granny Merrial would have been buried over there."

They all walked over, but the graves looked much too new.

Alice turned all around, a heavy weight in her chest. "Where is she?"

"Some reuse of land takes place, I believe," said Astrid. "She's sure to still be around here somewhere."

"Just somewhere?" said Alice, hands waving at the whole landscape.

"Probably just crumbs in the soil," said Astrid.

"At one with the earth," said Maddie, which sounded like a much nicer way of saying the same thing.

"My Granny Merrial was like your Uncle Kevin," said Alice. "Not a cripple, or one of them mobile problems, but I looked after her and she looked after me." She sighed. "There's no one there to look after my cow now."

"Now let's split up and find a really old grave," said Astrid brightly. "Let's aim for ... oh, let's say early eighteenth century. Bonus points if it has some sort of tomb lid that we can lift."

Astrid moved away, peering at the inscriptions. Maddie was about to go off in the other direction, but she glanced at Alice.

"Ah. I'm guessing that you don't read or write, Alice. Do you know numbers?"

"I knows numbers when they are things. I don't know the ways of numbers when they are not things."

"No worries. We can teach you that stuff. See here, these graves where your Granny Merrial was, they are all from the nineteen thirties." Maddy pointed at the figures. "One, nine, three, seven. Nineteen thirty-seven. We want one that is one, seven, something, something."

"Oh right. That seems easy enough." Alice skipped off. She headed for the more ancient looking stones. A few minutes later she found one. "Here!"

Maddie trotted over. "Great job, Alice! You're going to do great at numbers and reading. This one is seventeen twenty."

It took another twenty minutes before they found a grave from seventeen twenty three; clearly not the oldest, but it had the advantage of being a lidded tomb.

"So we reckon we can lift this then?" Alice said.

"We should test the weight now," Astrid said.

They positioned themselves around the tomb, fingertips under the edge of the cold stone lid.

"When I say go, we just try to lift it a tiny, tiny bit," said Astrid. "Go."

They lifted, and the stone shifted with a grinding sound. They put it down again. Alice watched carefully for any hint of unclean vapours escaping from the grave. The old superstitions were not easy to shake off.

"There we are then!" Astrid said, pleased. "So if we go back to seventeen thirty or so, we know we can use this place."

They walked through the graveyard, Astrid in high spirits because her plan was underway.

"Okay, so we go back to seventeen thirty," said Maddie. "Are we travelling salespeople who want to exchange some amazing gloves and belts for silver teapots? Who would go for that?"

Astrid wagged a finger. "Yes – we need to be more targeted. We present ourselves ... to the housekeeper of a large residence, perhaps. We show them our finery and ask if there are any household items which might be surplus to requirements."

Alice glanced at Astrid. It sounded like a really terrible plan, but Alice had little knowledge of big houses.

11

They sat on the bench at the side of the churchyard and Maddie took out the bag of wool scraps they'd retrieved from the compost bin near the allotments.

"So," said Maddie doling the stuff out. "If we assume it's the wool that gives us the power to travel in time – and I know how bonkers that sounds – then we should all be able to fashion ourselves a bracelet and be able to jump through time.

Alice was swiftly reducing the scraps to individual strands and plaiting them together.

"You don't think there's something in the manner in which they were constructed that gives them the power?" suggested Astrid.

"Mine was made by Gregory. He's a jobless physics graduate – not a trainee wizard."

"There's magic in certain knots," said Alice absently.

"I thought you weren't a witch."

"I'm not. Don't mean there's not magic in knots."

Soon they had three passable bracelets, and still plenty of scraps left over.

"Time to test them I guess," said Maddie.

Alice nodded and promptly vanished.

"What the fuck!" said Maddie. Before the final word had left her mouth, Alice was back in place on the bench.

Alice frowned. "Did it work?"

"Yuh-huh," said Maddie, stunned.

"You just focused, did you?" said Astrid. She stood. "Right." She breathed out and shook herself like an Olympic gymnast about to tackle a difficult routine. "Right. Right."

"Nervous?" Maddie suggested.

"No. I just—" She vanished.

Maddie sat and watched and waited.

"She's just jumped ahead a little while," said Alice.

"Yes."

And they waited some more. Three full minutes passed according to Maddie's phone. "What would be the funniest thing to do before she returns?" she said, talking to fight the growing nervousness she felt.

"What do you mean?" said Alice.

"Like, if we had time, we could have ourselves made up to look really, really old and then say to Astrid, 'Hello, dearie, we've been sat waiting on this bench for the last fifty years, waiting for you to return.'"

"Oh, I see. A jape. Yes, that would be funny." Alice's face tensed. "She has been gone a goodly while now."

"Yes."

"You don't think she has got lost?"

"Like trapped in the time vortex?"

"Is that a thing?" said Alice.

"I dunno, I just made it up. What if she never turns up? Do we call the police or—"

With no sound at all, Astrid was back again. "—want to psych myself up," she said, then looked at them. "It worked?"

"It did," said Maddie, trying not to sound relieved.

TOGETHER, they made their jump forward to Saturday morning once more, and loitered on the corner of Acacia Crescent until they saw the earlier versions of Astrid, Maddie and Alice go walking off from the house in the direction of the Baslow road petrol station.

"What would we do if we saw ourselves?" said Alice.

"We are seeing ourselves," said Astrid.

"I mean, like if we were the earlier selves and we saw ourselves come wandering by."

"Well, I suppose I'd just wave a jaunty greeting and say, 'Well met, fellow traveller,'" said Astrid.

"In that pretentious voice?" said Maddie.

"Nothing wrong with formal English," Astrid sniffed.

The trio of past selves were turning the corner.

"Why do I slouch like that?" said Maddie, regarding herself critically.

Astrid smiled. "Notice how I work proud and erect. I'm a fine figure of a woman." walk

Alice smirked. "Are you smitten with yourself, Mistress Astrid?"

Astrid tilted her head. "Nothing wrong with some high self-regard."

They walked towards the house. As they stepped onto the driveway, a band of figures appeared in the front garden. It was themselves: Alice, Maddie and Astrid. And for some reason, they had a brown cow with them.

"That's my cow," said Alice, astonished.

The Alice and Maddie on the lawn were hissing in argument. "Clearly too early! This is last week before Astrid did her Lady Gaga thing!"

Astrid raised her hand. "Well met, fellow travellers."

The Astrid on the lawn raised her hand in reply. "Well, met."

And then they were gone again.

Astrid turned to the others. "Like that, see?"

INDOORS, an hour later, Maddie looked around her and wondered at the situation she'd got herself into. The three women stood in Astrid's living room, dressed in what Astrid insisted were appropriate clothes. Alice had changed back into the washed and dried things she had worn in her own time. It had taken some convincing to get her out of her new stretchy leggings.

Maddie and Astrid wore vaguely similar garments which Alice had had fun fashioning for them. She insisted that being pinned into clothes was normal and declared that the curtain lining was very fine linen indeed. A woollen skirt and a shawl felt like bag lady levels of overkill, but Alice seemed happy. Maddie's Brownie blanket was getting another outing, but she made sure that the badges were inside.

"We're travelling to a time a hundred years after Alice's time," said Maddie. "Are you sure this is appropriate?"

"Fashions were slow to change. Even now, people can be seen wearing clothes that were fashionable sixty years ago."

"You need to be more dirty, mind," said Alice. "Your cleanliness is unnatural."

Astrid ran a finger along the top of a door and patted the dust onto her face as if she was applying a powder puff. "I've got a carrier bag fastened under my skirt," she said. "I suggest the two of you do the same, so we can carry what we need, out of sight."

"This is all completely crazy," said Maddie.

"We're all ready to go?" said Astrid.

Maddie pinned the bag of left-over time wool inside her baggy undergarments. "I believe we are."

They all held hands.

"Seventeen thirties," said Astrid. Instantly they were stumbling apart inside what appeared to be a huge gorse bush.

"Ow!" cried Alice, pulling herself free.

Maddie was grateful she had worn trainers on her feet, insisting that nobody would see them under the layers of peasant clothing – or bag lady chic as she was now mentally labelling it. The thorny bush snagged at her as she wrestled her way clear of it.

"Well, I guess this is what was here before my house,"

said Astrid. A couple of low buildings sat nearby. If they were in the twenty-first century they might be dens or allotment sheds, but Maddie guessed that people lived in them.

Maddie looked at her phone. The time and data hadn't changed. The only difference was a No Service message had come up.

"What was in the cloud before people connected the internet to it?" she mused absently.

"You are a moron," said Astrid. She gazed about. "Those places are no good for us," she said, waving at the buildings.

"Where will we find a big house?" said Maddie.

"We'll head for Burnley Manor," said Astrid.

They walked in what seemed like the correct direction.

"We're sure this is the seventeen hundreds?" said Maddie.

"'Tis a much bigger town than in the time I was born," said Alice.

Seen in bright daylight, eighteenth century Wirkswell barely looked big enough to be a town at all. There were buildings clustered along the river, the church on the hill, and some other buildings beyond, but it was a town without the sprawl of houses Maddie would have expected.

"How do you know where the road is?" she asked. "There's mud at the side and mud in the middle. Is a road just a line of mud? I thought they had cobblestones in the olden days?"

Astrid probably knew the answer to that, but she was preoccupied with taking in their surroundings. She was inhaling it greedily. "The smells! What is that? It's like woodsmoke mixed with something else."

"Shit?" Alice suggested.

They trudged on, Maddie wondering if the eighteenth century was just wall to wall mud. Then, as they moved into the town itself, they did come upon a more solid surface underfoot. "Cobbles!" Maddie instantly slipped and fell over into the mud.

"What on earth are you playing at?" Astrid hissed. "We are supposed to be blending in."

Maddie got to her feet, plastered thoroughly in the stinky mud.

"Now you really look like you belong," murmured Alice.

12

—————

Carriages rolled past them in both directions on the road to Burnley Manor, as if it was the only destination worth travelling to or from.

"Well this is splendid," said Astrid. "Let's see if we can find the kitchen door and put our plan into action."

Burnley Manor in seventeen-whatever was pretty much the same building which had survived into the twenty-first century. It was built from local stone, with large windows and doors. Many of the houses they had passed on their way were quainter, more primitive structures, but Maddie thought this one looked much more like a regular house, although on a grand scale.

There were many people inside and outside, all of them rushing about. A man in a fancy jacket with loads of buttons saw them dawdling about and shouted over at them. "Get around the back immediately! Guests will be here shortly and I won't have delivery wenches getting in the way!"

They scurried off in the direction indicated.

"Wenches?" whispered Astrid, indignantly.

"See?" said Maddie. "You don't like it when people use era-appropriate terminology to describe you."

Astrid stopped a small boy rushing in the opposite direction. He carried an empty wicker basket smelling of fish. "Hey, boy. Are they having a party in here?"

The boy nodded. "'Tis the Spring Ball."

Astrid straightened. "Many guests will be here, yes?"

He nodded again.

"If a fine lady wanted to attend the ball, where might she find a suitable carriage?" Astrid asked him.

The boy held out his hand in the unmistakeable gesture of someone who was saying no more unless he was rewarded for it.

Astrid sighed and turned her back to fiddle under her skirts. She withdrew a small keyring with a carved wooden koala attached to it, dangling it in front of the boy. "This will be yours, but I need to know that you will help me and my companions this evening."

The boy nodded wildly, his eyes alight. "Back of the smithy. My uncle the smith has made good a broken wheel, but it won't be collected until Sunday next."

"Go there and wait. We will join you later. Tell your uncle that he will be amply rewarded."

The boy ran off and Astrid grinned at Maddie and Alice.

"We don't know any fine ladies," said Alice, staring around in case there might be one she hadn't noticed.

"I think Astrid has a plan which involves her being one," said Maddie.

"That is correct. Of the three of us, I have the more noble bearing."

"And what part will Alice and I play in this plan?" Maddie asked.

"I will need footmen," said Astrid. "It might sound as if I am sidelining you, but it's essential that you operate the getaway vehicle."

Maddie rolled her eyes. "*Even if* you could blag your way into that party – which you can't because you're dressed up like a horrible baggage – are you seriously proposing to rob them of their silverware? They used to hang people for stuff like that, Astrid!"

"You misunderstand me," said Astrid. "Stealing things is definitely not the preferred option. I have an idea for trading which takes things up several notches."

Maddie and Alice looked at each other in frustration.

"Do share your new idea, Astrid," Maddie said. "Because we haven't even tried the old one yet."

"Come with, come with!" Astrid shepherded them both to the kitchen door. They opened it. The noise inside was the frantic shouting of a kitchen going at full pelt to deliver complex and numerous dishes at scale.

"Who do we even need to speak to?" Maddie asked.

"Is the housekeeper here?" shouted Astrid in her loudest teacher voice. "I need to speak with the housekeeper."

A red faced woman strode forward and faced them down, an angry expression on her face. "What's this? Busy times within and I'm timewasting with slatterns! Be off."

"One moment!" Astrid held up a hand. "Do you know what a pineapple is?"

The woman hesitated. "That I do, although we don't get them so much."

"Have you ever seen a real one?" Astrid persisted.

The woman licked her lips. She knew she would be at a disadvantage if she admitted the truth. "Not for some time," she said eventually.

"My mistress is in possession of three fine specimens. She has asked me to secure a good price for them."

"Three? That is surely not—"

"Three. 'Twould be a fine centrepiece for a ball. She will need a very good price, for there is much interest from elsewhere. Fine silverware is my mistress's particular weakness."

The housekeeper drew herself up. "I will send for the house steward. Can we see the goods?"

"My mistress is mindful of security. These are high value items. She will arrive here in a carriage if she receives the signal that conditions are favourable. We will need sight of the payment, naturally. Silverware of good quality will turn her head. It can be out of fashion if it is solid and interesting."

The housekeeper thought for a moment. "There is a set which has been little used of late. I will speak with the house steward. Send for your mistress. What name should we expect?"

"It will be Lady Gaga of, um, Motown."

"Very good." The housekeeper closed the door.

"What about that then?" Astrid said as she turned to the others, pumping the air with her fist.

"So we just need to go back, buy pineapples, find rich

person clothes for you, footman livery for us, then come back here, hire a carriage, do the deal, and hide the silverware in the grave," said Maddie, deadpan.

"What's a pineapple?" asked Alice.

"One of those big spikey fruits at the greengrocers," said Maddie.

"And people will pay silver just to own one?"

"We'll get a spare so you can try it later," said Astrid. "Come on now, chop chop."

13

The pineapples poked their spiky fronds out of the carrier bag as they left the greengrocer.

They had jumped back to the present together, realising they had jumped back to the opposite side of town to Astrid's house in oldy-timey clothes so had to avoid the stares of passersby before getting to Acacia Crescent, changing back into normal clothing and heading into town to buy the pineapples.

"'Tis a prickly beggar," Alice noted, jostling the pineapples in their bag.

Now, Astrid knew she would have to reveal the next part of her plan. She also knew the others wouldn't like it. "So our next stop is the museum," she said lightly. "They have everything that we need."

"That place we was thrown out of?" Maddie asked.

"Yes. We were thrown out," said Astrid.

"What on earth do you have in mind? And please tell me

it's not rooted in some petty vendetta you have with the woman at the museum."

"Of course it isn't. Irma Kidson is entirely beneath my interest," Astrid lied. "But I do know the exhibits well. There is a ball gown from the correct period, and some fancy jackets that will do for footmen. We are simply going to borrow them while the museum is closed. We can get them back before they open."

"Oh. We're just adding breaking and entering to our to-do list?" asked Maddie. "Are you out of your mind?"

"It won't be as hard as you think," said Astrid. "There is a little storeroom with a lock that yields to a hefty kick. We go in there and wait until they're closed."

"Not if they sees you coming," said Alice.

"Ah, but they won't!" Astrid pulled her master stroke. She had a pair of sunglasses and a large-brimmed hat folded in her bag. She whipped them out and showed them her instant disguise. "Ta da!"

"Oh, where did Astrid go?" asked Alice, looking all around with exaggerated movements.

"Did they have sarcasm in your time, or have you picked it up since you got here?" Astrid asked.

Alice shrugged.

Astrid guessed that simple people in the seventeenth century would have lacked the vocabulary to put a name to sarcasm. She couldn't resist being a schoolteacher again for a moment. "Sarcasm is where we say the opposite of what we mean in order to be offensive or amusing."

Alice gave a wide grin. "Oh, in that case, I am well versed in your sarcasm."

"Astrid, we will come along with you on this increasingly insane trip," Maddie said. "But we should get some sandwiches if we are going to be locked in a cupboard for hours

"Good idea," said Astrid.

Astrid's disguise proved surprisingly successful at the museum entrance and she swaggered through the building. It was irritating that she couldn't see properly because the lenses of the sunglasses were really quite dark, but the triumph of being undetected made up for it.

"It's about forty five minutes before closing," said Maddie. "We should all use the facilities before we shut ourselves away."

"Use what facilities?" Alice asked.

"The toilets. We should take a piss," said Maddie. "What would it be called in your time?"

"Oh I reckon we'd have a dozen ways of saying that," cackled Alice. "We would say leak or piss. But then we had Tom down the road who would tell us he was filling up the cuckoo pint when he went in the hedge."

"Cuckoo pint?" Maddie asked.

"'Tis a plant. Surely you know it? Has a goblet for a flower." Alice formed her hands into the shape. "And a ruddy great stick up the middle – like a poker."

Astrid realised she knew the plant. "Lords and ladies, yes!"

Alice beamed. "Right let's use the facilities."

A few minutes later, Astrid showed them the cupboard. "Here we are. Flimsy lock, I can just open it with a quick shove. Watch the door."

Alice and Maddie gave her the all-clear and Astrid shoulder-barged the door. She bounced off, while the door stood firm. She tried again with the same result.

"Well. Either I have grown weaker since I last did this or they have replaced the lock," Astrid said. "There's nothing else for it." She beckoned to Maddie and Alice.

Maddie shook her head. "You're right, we should bail on this and go back to yours."

"No! Come here and help me break down this door! With all three of us, we should be able to do it."

Maddie and Alice exchanged a glance. Reluctantly, they joined her.

"Right, get in position. We must all use as much force as we can put into it," said Astrid.

"Not being funny, Astrid, but how can we even all fit? Three people can't fit a doorway," said Maddie.

"We'll need to spoon. It's got to be like a spooning barge. There, I just invented a thing. Maybe one day the Olympic Games will include the spooning barge, but right now we're winging it. We start a step back, all spooning, then we count down and lunge sideways in perfect synchronisation – barging our shoulders at the door."

"Oh, spooning! Like spoons!" Alice said. The word clearly pleased her.

"You can go in the middle then," said Maddie.

"Fine!" said Astrid. "Come on. Let's do one practice go to get the steps right, then we'll go for real. All squash together. When we get to three we step and *blam!*"

They stepped through a rehearsal and, confident they were all working together, they delivered the real blow. The door smashed open and they tumbled into the cupboard space.

"Flipping heck, we broke the frame!" said Maddie, pointing at splintered wood.

"It's on the inside, nobody will see with the door shut," said Astrid, fumbling for the light switch. She pushed the door closed and held it in place with a step ladder from the corner.

They all stood for a moment, making sure that the crashing noise hadn't brought museum staff running.

"I think we're fine," said Astrid. "Now, I spy some boxes of paper. Let's drag them out and get comfy."

They all made stools from boxes and ate their sandwiches.

"Slices of bread with cheese or meat in between," said Alice, peeling back the layers to investigate. "'Tis a pretty arrangement."

They were in there a full half hour before Alice said. "Hang on. Are we just waiting for them to lock up?"

"We are," said Astrid.

"Then why don't we just leap forward in time a few hours?"

"Well—" Astrid huffed and sighed. "Maybe ... we shouldn't use time travel frivolously and recognise the virtue of patience."

"Are you just saying that because you hadn't thought of it yourself?" said Maddie.

Astrid huffed "It was a good idea to break in here and wait."

"Or we could have just come in and jumped forward. No

need for breaking in at all."

"The plan was sound!"

"Oh, yeah, yeah," said Maddie, grabbing each of the others by the wrist. Their arrival in the same spot, later in the evening, was imperceptible.

"I would have happily waited," said Astrid.

"And I realise I'll never have to actually wait for takeaway to be delivered ever again," said Maddie. "Make the order, leap forward, and collect instantly."

Astrid made a dubious sound. "I think we might venture forth and find our outfits, now."

They made their way through the museum. Maddie's phone torch was helpful in lighting the way.

"This way, we want the Georgian display room," said Astrid.

They entered the room and Astrid smiled as she saw the dress she had planned to wear. It was a heavy brocade silk, featuring huge pink camellia flowers and leaves that twirled across its voluminous, panniered skirt. "Look! This is so perfect for the occasion. It's so very Georgian!"

"It's so very *small*. There's no way that will fit you, Astrid," said Maddie.

"Nonsense. Where there's a will, there's a way." Although Astrid did think it looked a little tight around the waist.

After they had wrestled it off its stand, Astrid attempted to get into it, along with the voluminous underskirts and the odd basketwork supports at the sides.

"What are those things?" Maddie asked. "It's like you've got an umbrella stand tied to each hip!"

"They are panniers to give the dress support for that wide

silhouette," said Astrid. "Now, will it do up, that is the question?"

"Er, no," said Maddie. "There is quite a gap around the fastenings."

"You'll be wanting some stays," said Alice, pointing at Astrid's middle.

"Yes, of course!" said Maddie. "Does the museum have stuff like that?"

"Try the Victorian room next door," said Astrid.

Maddie ran back in a few minutes later. "This looks like a proper instrument of torture. I reckon this will sort you out."

Astrid huffed and grumbled as she was trussed up in the unforgiving whalebone of the corset. Maddie and Alice had less sympathy than she would have liked as they heaved and pummelled her flesh into shape, but Astrid was prepared to overlook all of that when the dress finally fastened over her altered form.

"Looks good?" she wheezed. She needed to get used to the constriction.

"Yeah," said Maddie, doing a circuit. "Isn't your hair supposed to be different too?"

"Wig," said Astrid, waving a hand in the direction of a display case.

Maddie opened a cabinet. "Ew. Not sure I'd want this on my head." She carried it over at arm's length. "What on earth does it smell of?"

"Mothballs," said Astrid. "It will be fine. Help me get it on, then go and get those jackets and hats from over there."

Alice went over to look. "Proper finery! We will look so fancy in these, Maddie."

Astrid tottered around in a tiny circle. She had quickly dismissed the Georgian shoes as being way too small, so she had trainers on underneath the huge dress, but movement was not easy.

"When you need to use the facilities you will need to piss on the floor I reckon," said Alice.

"The olden times are just gross, aren't they?" said Maddie.

"I gather there were small boys with pots back in the day," said Astrid. "I will just need to hold on. Now, jackets on you two. We need you to look passable. I will be the one who is under most scrutiny."

Maddie and Alice shrugged on jackets and placed tricorn hats on their heads.

"Looking very dapper ladies. Now we shall return to claim our coach and take our pineapples to the ball!"

"Where did you put the gloves and other things that we will need to trade?" Maddie asked. "Or do your footmen need to carry all of this stuff?"

"If you don't mind!" Astrid gave an imperious wave of her hand, feeling her way into the role.

14

If Maddie had thought normal Astrid could be insufferable, she needed a new word to describe Astrid in her new role as Lady Gaga of Motown. Even the name made no sense; but Astrid had fully embraced the idea that she was now a member of the aristocracy who could order others about as her servants.

They had travelled back to find the smithy, and the carriage they could hire for the evening. The boy they had spoken to earlier appeared around a corner at the sound of their voices, beckoning them towards a low shed.

"Uncle, 'tis the ladies who have need of a carriage."

The smith was a broad-chested man wearing a huge coarse apron. He looked at the three of them, apparently unfazed by the sight of Astrid's giant gown and two obviously female footmen.

"I cannot have damage to this carriage, understand? You know well how to handle such things?"

"Of course!" said Astrid. "Let me show you the payment we have for you. It should put your mind at ease. We have brought you precious items from afar." She held out a hand to indicate Maddie should bring forth the charity shop offerings.

Maddie held out each item as if it was a wedding ring on a velvet cushion.

"A pair of ladies' gloves. They are made from Thinsulate, which keeps the hands very warm. A men's leather belt. A pair of slipper socks. They have special grippy parts on the base so you don't slip on the floor. A set of men's handkerchiefs. A ladies' scarf, printed with horses. A small plastic dish printed with an image of Bournemouth." She turned to the boy. "Here is your koala keyring, of course, and also some crayons and a colouring book."

The boy took the things, wide-eyed, and ran off with them. Only as he left did Maddie realise that the koala keyring looked awfully like an ancient pendant she was pretty sure she'd seen in the local museum.

"Are we messing with history here?" she whispered.

Astrid shushed her violently.

The smith was transfixed by the image of Bournemouth on the cheap plastic dish. It was a cheap seaside souvenir from way before Maddie's time, if the yellowed plastic was any guide, but photographs would not be something the smith had ever encountered, so it probably looked very unusual.

He waved them onwards, shouting for the boy to return and help with the horses.

A few minutes later the carriage was ready to go, a pair of

horses attached at the front. The boy placed a stool for Astrid to climb into the carriage. Maddie drifted along behind, but the smith waved towards the front of the carriage.

"Up you go then lads!"

Maddie looked at the seat high on the front of the carriage and realised footmen were expected to sit up there and drive the horses. Her first problem was going to be climbing up. How on earth was she supposed to do that without a ladder? She hesitated for a moment, but realised she needed to project confidence, so she stepped up onto a ledge and scrambled the rest of the way up. When she was up on the narrow seat she looked down, and wished she hadn't. It really didn't feel safe. But she smiled and slid over so Alice could sit beside her.

"Any idea what we are supposed to do?" she whispered to Alice.

Alice shook her head.

"'Tis a cloudy night. Young Sam will accompany you with a link!" shouted the smith.

Maddie and Alice looked blankly at each other, before realising that a link was a light as the boy trotted ahead of them holding a flaming torch to light the way.

"We want the reins then?" murmured Maddie. She conjured a vague picture of cowboy films where twitching reins and shouting "Yee haw!" would make the horses do their thing.

She gathered the only strips of leather she could see and held them taut. She coughed lightly and gave them a flick. "Come on then!"

Whether the horses followed the light of the torch

rather than what Maddie was attempting to do with the reins, she would never know. Either way they only travelled a little way down the road before the horses slowed to a halt.

"Samuel!" shouted Maddie. "Can you please come and help?"

The boy walked back. They agreed that he would drive the horses, helping Alice to understand how it was done, while Maddie held the torch to light the way.

She trudged through the endless mud, somewhat resentful of Astrid riding in the comfortable interior. She lit the way to Burnley Manor, all the while fearful that the torch thing was going to set her on fire.

As the carriage made its way around a looped driveway, a man in a much more formal version of Maddie's scruffy footman ensemble approached them.

"Would this be Lady Gaga of Motown?"

"Yes, sir."

"Very good. The house steward wishes to meet her ladyship. He will be here presently."

They were guided to one side while other carriages pulled up to drop off their occupants.

Maddie went round to the carriage door to give Astrid the message.

"He's coming out here?" Astrid demanded.

"Yes. That's what we want, isn't it?" Maddie asked.

"I was rather hoping to attend the ball," said Astrid. "Help me down from here. I shall make my entrance and he can find me."

"No! What on earth are you doing? We can't split up! The

plan only works if you stay here, we do the deal, then we all leave together with the loot."

Astrid huffed and grunted as she tried to work out how to climb down while she was wearing the enormous gown. "It's a plan that can flex as we want it to."

"Why do we want it to flex? Do you just want to go to the ball so you can swank around in your fancy frock?"

"Yes! How often do we get to observe history this closely? It will be a chance to meet the Burnley family and see what they're like!"

"No! This is not the time to indulge your historical nosiness. You can make a separate trip to do that, surely?"

"One needs to be dressed up as aristocracy to hobnob with aristocracy," said Astrid, in her most condescending tone. "It will be a small delay with few risks to the original plan. You and Alice will be welcomed by the household staff, I am sure."

With that, Astrid managed to flop across the seat and squirm on her belly so that her feet extended over the doorway of the carriage. A half second later she stood on the ground, looking smug. She straightened her gown and headed off at speed to join the other guests entering the building.

"Lady Gaga of Motown? I was led to believe that she would be meeting with me to arrange a trade."

Maddie turned as she heard the new voice. It was the house steward: an older man, wearing a more subdued frock coat in dark grey.

"She has joined the guests, sir, but we may conclude the deal here if you wish."

Alice jumped down to join her in a welcome show of solidarity. There was certainly a risk he would simply seize the pineapples and send them on their way.

Maddie thought she saw the idea flit briefly behind his eyes; then he smiled and beckoned them forward. "Very well. Show me the goods."

Maddie drew in a breath. "And you sire, also have, um, goods?" She wasn't sure she was getting the language right, but surely the nature of deal making hadn't changed much over the years.

He looked ready to berate her impertinence, but breathed out a tired sigh instead. He beckoned to a boy waiting in the shadows, who brought forward a bulging canvas bag.

The house steward raised his eyebrows and held open the bag. Maddie dipped a hand in and pulled out a large silver tray. It was heavy and looked very fancy to her eyes. If it wasn't what Astrid wanted, tough. She'd gone off and left them.

Maddie reached inside the carriage and retrieved the Tesco carrier bag with the pineapples. She held it open for the house steward. He put his face over the bag and inhaled deeply.

"The smell of rot is absent," he murmured in approval. He pulled out one of the pineapples and ran his hands over the surface. "It is firm indeed."

Maddie nodded. "All is in order then?"

He nodded back and they exchanged the two bags.

"Since your mistress has joined the other guests, might I

suggest that you come and have a light supper in the kitchen while you wait for her?" he said.

Maddie had planned to wait it out in the carriage, but Astrid might be hours. She glanced up at Alice who shrugged.

"Yes. Thank you."

They followed the house steward around the building into the kitchen. Maddie clutched the canvas bag firmly to her side.

"You will be well looked after in here," he said. "Now I have other matters to attend to." He took the pineapples and left Maddie and Alice on a bench near the fire.

"Mug of grog, my sweets?" asked a woman in a white cloth cap.

They both gave eager nods.

15

Astrid walked through the entrance hall of Burnley Manor, soaking up every detail. The decor was less sombre than stately homes tended to be in more modern times. Yellow was cheerfully applied to walls and curtains, and enormous arrangements of flowers teetered on many surfaces.

She slipped her phone out from its place up her sleeve and very discreetly took some snaps of her surroundings. She could see that other guests were checking her out. In fact, there was some definite gossiping which seemed to involve her – much fluttering of fans, masking fingers pointed in her direction. Had they seen her phone? Perhaps her arrival had caused a stir. She hoped it was the good kind, where all of the most eligible men would insist upon dancing with her to find out more. She glanced around, wishing she had a fan of her own, so that she could pose mysteriously.

She strolled slowly forward, admiring paintings as she

went. She climbed a short staircase and followed the noise towards what was surely the main ballroom.

"I'm sorry madam, but I cannot permit you to enter!" A butler was at her elbow, looking sorrowful but firm.

"Whyever not? My name is on the guestlist, surely? Lady Gaga of Motown?"

"It is a matter more delicate in nature. Permit me to show you?" He led her along a corridor that skirted the ballroom. Astrid could hear the jollity from within and was frustrated by the delay in joining them.

"In here madam, and you will understand the most vexing situation."

There was a discreet balcony with a view of the ballroom. Astrid took a moment to absorb the sights and sounds. There was a smell too: a curious mixture of heavy perfume laced with the sharp tang of sweat. A small group of musicians occupied the far end of the room, playing something lively on violins. Those dancing moved in a carefully choreographed manner. Astrid realised she would never be able to join in with the more formal dances. If she couldn't shake off this butler, she wouldn't be doing any dancing at all.

He coughed lightly. "Lady Burnleigh can clearly be seen below the large portrait of her father near the eastern door. Next to her husband there."

Astrid leaned over to see where he was pointing and her jaw dropped. "Shit!" she breathed.

"Indeed, madam."

The woman was wearing Astrid's dress. It actually was Lady Burnleigh's dress. Astrid was wearing the same dress, but from the future. This was probably very bad.

Maddie had made all sorts of fuss about them meeting themselves while they were time travelling, and Astrid recognised there could be unforeseen consequences. What about a dress, though?

Stunned but enthralled, Astrid slipped out her phone and snapped a picture of the woman down in the ballroom.

"It is my understanding that Lady Burnleigh is greatly invested in leading the way in the latest and most exclusive fashions," the butler was saying. "She brought the fashion for floral mantuas to Derbyshire."

"Did she now?"

"She cannot see you wearing that dress."

"I think it might be a bit too late for that," said Astrid.

Lady Burnleigh had frozen in horror, her eyes fixed on Astrid. For a long moment, they stared at each other, then Lady Burnleigh waved over a footman and whirled towards the door. It crossed Astrid's mind that Lady Burnleigh would be more accustomed to moving around in these crippling garments. She hoped it would not require a running race.

"Quickly," said the butler. "You need to leave now."

"My carriage is at the front—"

"I shall conduct you to the rear of the house, where there is less chance of an unfortunate meeting."

He ushered her along another corridor and to a much smaller staircase, which was very awkward to navigate with the exaggerated width of the basketwork panniers across her hips. She kept bumping into the sides and having to swivel as she went.

"I will need my footmen!" yelled Astrid as she tottered along yet another corridor.

"I believe they are receiving refreshments in the kitchen," said the butler.

"To the kitchen then!" Astrid said.

"Alas, every moment you remain within this house—"

"Enough!" Astrid bellowed. "I understand that her ladyship doesn't want to see me wearing a dress like hers, but seriously! You're acting as if I've stolen her firstborn!"

The butler held up his hands and adopted a placatory tone. "I merely wished to avoid unpleasantness, but if you wish to visit the kitchen then I shall take you there."

Astrid could smell the kitchen before they reached it. There were delicious food smells and the sounds of many people working together. When they arrived, she looked around for Maddie and Alice.

The butler asked a passing maid and she nodded to a bench seat with a small smile. "Fast asleep, sir!"

Astrid went over. "Maddie! Alice!"

They did not stir. Each held a half-empty tankard. Astrid shook them both by their shoulders, but they just mumbled and did not open their eyes.

"Someone has roofied them—!" Astrid remembered herself. "Someone has administered a sleeping draught!"

There was no sign of the pineapples or of any silverware.

"Where is the house steward?" Astrid demanded.

The butler looked confused. "What business do you have with the house steward?"

"I demand to speak with him. I believe he has reneged on a deal I made regarding some fine pineapples!"

"Now now, Lady Gaga. I am sure there has been some misunderstanding. There are no pineapples hereabouts."

Astrid saw the looks exchanged between several of the kitchen staff. "Look! They know about the pineapples! Ask them!"

The butler looked as if he was out of his depth. His stiff and formal manner could not disguise the fact that he had no firm grip on the facts. He glanced around and nobody would meet his eye. Another man entered the kitchen and the butler visibly sagged with relief. "Sir. The lady has been asking for you."

The house steward stepped forward. "I gather you have been causing something of a disturbance?" he said to Astrid.

Astrid drew herself up to her full height. "You will not speak to me in that tone, my man! I came here in good faith to trade the most beautiful pineapples, and I find that you have drugged my assistants in order to dupe me. It is an outrage!"

"An outrage?" said the house steward softly. "I believe Lady Burnleigh has a different view on what we might call *an outrage*."

He stepped aside and Lady Burnleigh entered the room. Her face was a mask of rage. Beneath the mask was a woman who was perhaps using a bit too much lead-based make up to hide her advancing middle age.

"I can barely believe my eyes," Lady Burnleigh said, pointing at Astrid's dress. "It is too much to imagine that this be mere coincidence. Who sent you here? Who wishes to demean me in this way? I paid a London seamstress for an original dress!"

Astrid had no answer to that, so she decided that her best defence was a sound offence. "A dress is merely a dress, madam, but I must take issue with the poisoning of my colleagues!" She pointed at Maddie and Alice. "I came here to make an honest trade for some pineapples and they have been attacked in my absence."

"Why would you think such a thing?" said the house steward. "They have simply had too much ale. Half-cut before they arrived, I'll wager."

Astrid bridled. This man was not only trying to swindle her, but he was also trying to portray them all as drunken idiots.

"So where is my payment then? You have the pineapples, where is my payment?"

The house steward leaned across and whispered loudly to Lady Burnleigh. "Not right in the head m'lady. I'll have her escorted off the premises."

"Yes." She gave Astrid an appraising look. "However, I do not want her to leave while she wears that dress."

"What? No!" Astrid backed away from them and nearly bumped into a maid carrying a jug of milk.

Could they possibly be serious? Astrid snatched the jug from the maid and poured it over Maddie and Alice.

"Wake up! These people have all gone mad, we need to leave!"

Maddie and Alice stirred groggily, but their eyes flickered only briefly. Astrid grunted with frustration. If she grabbed them now could she jump them back to their own time?. She also had to admit that she had only the sketchiest understanding of how the time travelling worked. Maddie seemed reasonably proficient at getting them where they needed to go, but Astrid wasn't certain she had mastered the finer points herself. She couldn't risk them all ending up in the Bronze Age; or worse, Astrid ending up in the Bronze Age alone. She ran across the kitchen, heedless of the enormous dress – which swept bowls off tables as she barged past. She would dearly love to be able to shed those panniers, but they were very firmly tied in place underneath a multitude of layers. She ran through the kitchen door out into the night. She had no immediate plan beyond getting away from the people who wanted to strip her out of her clothes. As she ran into the darkness, a voice called.

"Astrid! Over here!"

From behind a topiary rabbit, Alice peered out and waved. There were two others with her. One was a very distressed-looking man in a tall black puritan hat. The other was a dun-coloured cow.

"You have a cow with you," said Astrid needlessly.

"This is Teasel," Alice grinned.

"By God!" swore the bearded man, upset and exasperated. "Another witch?"

"And this is Master Continent Berwick, the witchfinder who tried to have me burned."

"What?" said Astrid.

"The evidence of devilry mounts before my eyes!" the man cried.

"Shut up," snapped Astrid irritably and then looked back at Alice. "To repeat: What?"

16

By what little light was available, Astrid could see there were several people at the door of the house exploring the garden, so she ducked into the shadow of the sinister topiary.

"How can you be here?" she hissed to Alice.

"It's a long story." Alice seemed to have changed clothes, from one set of horrid peasant rags to another.

"Are these the gardens of hell?" the witchfinder demanded.

"The short version of the story, please," said Astrid.

"I went back in time."

"For a cow and witchfinder? Sorry – did you say his name was Continent?"

"An honest and God-fearing name," said the witchfinder.

Alice smiled. "I went back, used some mandies to make a sleeping draught, and gave the potion to the evildoers in the kitchen some time ago."

"Mandies?"

"Mandrax. That's right, isn't it? *I'm Mandy, Fly Me.*"

"Who ... who ... how do you know *I'm Mandy, Fly Me*?"

"You mentioned it."

"When?"

"Nineteen sixty-something. Time travel is very complicated."

Astrid had so many questions but decided to go for an easy one. "And how did you know which ones were the evildoers?"

Alice shrugged. "I assumed they all were. They should be sleeping very, very soon."

The two of them peered out as the pursuers clattered past. They could hear the house steward shouting instructions. It wasn't long before they saw people start to stumble and fall where they stood.

"Now," said Alice, "I can't help you with the next part, because I don't want to meet my other self. You need to go in there, attempt to steal the silverware that is rightfully ours, and get Maddie and the other Alice back out here. The carriage will be waiting. You have about fifteen minutes."

Astrid resented being bossed around, but Alice had a game plan, and it seemed solid. "Are you certain you drugged everyone? How do you even do a thing like that?"

Alice winked. "I did and I will show you later. No more dallying." She clapped her hands to convey urgency and, in an instant, vanished.

Continent Berwick staggered back. "Witchcraft!"

"Possibly," said Astrid. She crept back towards the house.

"Witch!" Continent called after her. "What is to become of me?"

"Not my problem!" Astrid called back and hurried to the house.

Astrid crept into the kitchen and found every single person unconscious, slumped on the floor or over a table. She hurried over to Alice and Maddie and shook them again. They stirred slightly, but not enough. Astrid looked around.

"Silverware, silverware..." She realised the good stuff was likely to be locked away. She trotted outside to find the unconscious form of the house steward, and located a large ring of keys hanging from his belt. She grabbed it and hurried back to the kitchen. She followed a likely trail of cupboards containing crockery and serving platters along a wall until she found a locked one. It took several precious minutes to find the correct key, but when the door swung open, she knew she had found what she needed. She grabbed a tablecloth and used it as a makeshift bag for her haul. It was tempting to take all of it, but Astrid wanted to honour the spirit of the original deal, so she only took half. She picked up the heavy, clanking parcel and felt instantly better. She hurried back to Maddie and Alice.

"Come on!" She slapped their faces and tugged at their arms. "Outside, quickly! There is no time to spare." They staggered to their feet and immediately fell down again, but Astrid was remorseless. "Come *on*!"

She shepherded them out into the night air, which revived them both enough to register that their faces really hurt from all the slapping.

"Wash oo do to us?" slurred Maddie, touching a hand to her cheek.

"Into the carriage!" Astrid said.

Samuel was waiting by the carriage, while the other Alice was nowhere to be seen. Astrid shoved Maddie and Alice inside and stashed the silverware on the floor.

"We need to get away from here as fast as we can, Samuel. Can you drive the carriage without someone to light the way?"

He gave a small nod. "Samuel Sykes at your service ma'am. Back into town?"

"Yes. But drop us off near the church, will you?"

The ride away from Burnley Manor was much more uncomfortable than their arrival. The carriage bounced through unseen potholes and swerved around corners at the higher speed, but at least they were putting distance between themselves and the staff who were probably waking up by now.

"Woo!" shouted Maddie, who was fully awake but clearly not quite back to normal.

They pulled up near to the church and all jumped down from the carriage.

Samuel was given additional payment in the form of a cloth purse shaped like a shark. He was delighted with it.

Astrid tried to carry the tablecloth bundle quietly, as it sounded exactly like she imagined a stolen haul of expensive silverware to sound. It would be very bad if anyone followed them into the graveyard and saw them hide it.

"Come on, let's find the grave!"

The graveyard was very different to its twenty-first

century version, especially in the dark. There were no paths, and even the church wasn't the same shape.

"Is it that one over there?" Alice said, pointing.

They all walked over. "It looks so new," said Maddie.

They were all thinking the same thing, Astrid was certain. Attempting to open a grave that was hundreds of years old was like archaeology. There was a detachment that came with the passage of time. When it was so new it felt more like a violation.

Astrid coughed. "We'd better get on with it. One on each side. We know we can do this."

She knew she would have no hands free when they lifted the lid, so she braced the silverware bundle on the right pannier of her dress, leaning it onto the edge of the tomb. She hoped that with a small swivel of her hips, she'd be able to pitch it inside once they'd made a decent gap.

"Are we up to this, ladies?" she asked.

There were mumbles of agreement.

"Right. We want to lift it up two hand spans. Ready? Go!"

They made a lot of noise lifting the lid. Maddie made a huffing noise, Alice roared and staggered. As they reached the height they were after, Astrid attempted her hip swivel. It was partially successful, as the bundle tipped forward, but it stuck halfway, not quite dropping through the gap.

"Keep lifting! Don't drop it!" she yelled. If only the panniers were a more useful shape! She tried to use the right side as a bat, but it was more of a wafting device, rather than the walloping one that she needed. She grunted with frustration as she tried to lift her knee to shove the bundle further in. It was a hopeless effort: there were countless layers of clothing preventing her knee from connecting. She slammed her whole body sideways, and felt something break and stab into her side. She dropped the slab as the searing pain tore through her.

"Fuck, Astrid! I nearly lost my fingers," shrieked Maddie.

Astrid clutched her side. "Christ. I need to get this fucking dress off before it kills me."

Alice and Maddie came towards her.

"There is much blood!" said Alice.

Astrid tried not to look at the blood on her hand when she touched her hip.

"We'll help you out of this," said Maddie. "Is it that basketwork thing that's stuck in you?"

It took much longer than Astrid would have liked before she stood free of the dress and its punishing foundation pieces. She looked at her injured side and hissed.

"Can we just get out of here?" said Maddie.

"Back to the present," Astrid nodded.

"I feel past, present and future have lost all meaning," said Alice, wearily.

Maddie grabbed both their hands and they jumped.

17

Another night in another Wirkswell.

Maddie didn't need to look at her phone to know they were back in their own time. Orange streetlights covered the town, filling the sky with their soft glow. Maddie held Astrid's dangerous dress over one arm. Despite the emergency undressing, the basketwork looked remarkably intact.

"Your wound needs dressing," said Alice. "I could make a poultice."

"I have a perfectly serviceable first aid kit at home," said Astrid.

"Good," said Maddie. "I could do with a sit down and a cuppa too."

"Not until we've taken our treasure," said Astrid, coughing meaningfully and tapping the tomb next to her.

They renewed their efforts on the grave. When the top of

the stone was slid across by a good six inches, Maddie and Astrid turned on their phone torches. Maddie peered into the depths, but could see nothing but clods of earth and a Haribo wrapper, which must have been posted through the tiny gap.

"Can you see anything?" Alice asked.

"No," said Maddie. The grave was empty.

"How is this possible?" said Astrid.

They spent several more minutes shining their torch beams into every part of the tomb, but it was just a box with very little to explore.

"Where is the actual coffin?" Maddie asked. "I sort of thought that would be in here."

"It's called a chest tomb. They bury the body underground then put this box-shaped thing over the top," said Astrid.

Alice gave a small raspberry of mockery at the wasted space.

They all gave up the search and grasped the lid.

"Close it up?" Maddie said miserably. The others nodded and they slid the lid back.

"Someone must have opened it in-between times," said Alice, slumping down on a nearby grave.

"Bastards," said Astrid, with feeling.

"Amen," said Maddie.

It was a slow and miserable waddle across town to Astrid's house. There, Maddie and Alice inspected Astrid's corsetry-inflicted wound.

"It's not that deep," said Maddie, as she cleaned the

wound and applied some steri strips from a first aid box. "It will be sore, but I don't think it's life threatening."

"Remarkable substances," said Alice, fingering the plasters and ointments in the first aid kit.

"All this pain for nothing," grumbled Astrid.

"Also," said Alice putting her hair to her nose. "Why do I smell of milk?"

"It's a long story," said Astrid. "I'm going to bed."

MADDIE WENT ROUND to Astrid's the following day. If she had used the time jumping bracelet to reward herself with another lie-in and a chance to shower the milky smell out of her hair, she wasn't going to tell anyone.

She had spent breakfast time with Uncle Kevin and her diary. In it, she tried to draw a timeline of their adventures into the past. She had covered a two page spread with dates, arrows and little stick figures before she felt it almost made sense. She gave Kevin a kiss on the forehead and walked over the Astrid's through the Sunday morning quiet of the town.

She found Astrid in her kitchen, still complaining long and loud about how they had been robbed. She interspersed that with complaints about the injury she had sustained, but she seemed to be moving about without any difficulty. Alice was drying her hair.

"Voluntarily taking a shower?" Maddie asked.

"'Tis not so bad once you get used to it," Alice conceded.

"Plans for the day?" said Maddie.

"Return the dress to the museum and work out what went wrong," said Astrid.

It was as good a plan as any. They walked down to Wirkswell Museum and went into the dingy little courtyard between it and the town hall that locals called Alice's Place.

"Because this is the spot where they tried to burn me?" said Alice.

"The very spot," said Maddie. "Now, we need to jump back to any point last week when the museum was open, don't we?"

She thought hard, the light of the sky flicked from one grey to another, and they went round to the entrance and in through the open door. Luckily, there was no one in the foyer, especially not Astrid's nemesis, Irma.

"And now we jump to that night when we stole the dress," said Alice. "After we stole it, of course."

"Borrowed," said Astrid.

"Three in the morning should do it," said Maddie and jumped.

Now all was darkness again, and they made their way through the building, back to the Georgian section.

There was the empty display. Alice pushed the pieces of the pannier over the mannequin. Maddie helped arrange the dress back on top, although it did look very soiled, with dirt, blood, and several large rips.

"Looking good," she said, with more optimism than honesty.

"Bugger me," whispered Astrid.

Maddie looked round. Astrid was shining her light on the small display about Burnbeck Mill.

"What is it?" said Alice.

Astrid read out what it said on one of the display panels. *"Samuel Atkins (1718-1770) was born into a poor family of blacksmiths. 'Lucky Sam' established the wool mill at Burnbeck, just below Continent Cave (home to a famed eighteenth century religious hermit). Samuel Atkins and the Burnbeck Mill helped bring the Industrial Revolution to the Wirkswell area."*

Alice stared at her. "What, little Samuel? The boy with the coach?"

Maddie nodded. "Little Samuel Atkins, who was born poor and got rich enough to be a mill owner somehow."

Alice's mouth dropped open. "He followed us that night!"

"Stole our silver."

"Cheeky blighter!" said Astrid. She angled her torch down to the blackened 'grotesque pendant' that was supposedly left behind by Samuel Atkins.

"That's a koala key fob," said Maddie. "Oh, wow, are we messing with history." She took out her diary and showed the others her mad scribbles. "This is us, travelling around, messing with history, here and there. We've only done – *pfff* – six jumps maybe and we're already rewriting local history."

"I must write down some thoughts before they slip away," said Astrid. "Such a valuable learning resource."

Maddie shuffled uncomfortably. "You would be careful how you did that though, wouldn't you? We're not going to see a self-published book called *My Time-Travelling Life* are we? That would be asking for trouble."

"Of course not," mumbled Astrid, as if that was exactly where her mind had been going. "I have taken some photos though."

"You did what?" said Maddie.

"For research purposes only." She held out her phone. "Look."

She flicked through photos she'd surreptitiously taken during her time inside Burnley Manor. "These could be invaluable for any historian of the period. See, this is Lady Burnleigh, wearing the exact same dress I turned up in."

Alice snatched at Astrid's wrist to hold it steady. "Go back to the last one," she said urgently.

"You are hurting my wrist," said Astrid.

"The last one!"

Astrid thumbed back. Alice audibly gasped.

"What is it?" said Maddie.

Alice tapped at the image on the screen. "That is Master Burnleigh."

"Yes, we know," said Astrid. "Lady Burnleigh and the alderman Master Burnleigh."

"No, you do not understand," said Alice, a strange tension suffusing her entire being. "This is seventeen hundred and some other number, but that man there, I know him. From my own time."

"Well, obviously, you can't," said Astrid. "This was taken a hundred years after your time."

"I tell you plainly, woman," said Alice, backing away. "That is the alderman I knew, the very man who condemned me to death. 'Tis Master Roger Burnleigh, I swear."

"Perhaps it's just a strong family resemblance – a great grandson or something," suggested Maddie, trying to bring some calm to the situation. But the expression on Alice's face, seen in the stark light of the phone's torch, made it clear the 'grandson' explanation was not going to cut it.

"What in God's name is going on?" Alice whispered.

"Clearly, we're not the only ones messing with time," said Astrid.

ABOUT THE AUTHOR

Heide Goody lives in North Warwickshire with her family and pets.

Iain Grant lives in South Birmingham with his family and pets.

They are both married, but not to each other.

ALSO BY HEIDE GOODY AND IAIN GRANT

Butts to the Future

The time-bending adventure series that brings history to life with humour, adventure and heart.

Maddie Waites, Astrid Bohart and Alice Hickenhorn have the power to travel through time. They decide to take a break from using this power to repeatedly save the life of a careless motorcyclist and embark on a trip back in time to steal valuable pop memorabilia from the swinging sixties before it becomes valuable.

However, it seems that adventures in the past comes with their own unexpected problems including time-travelling cows, mad-eyed witchfinders and the increasingly sinister Master Burnleigh.

These raucous and twisty novellas are perfect for fans of Jodi Taylor

Butts to the Future

Clovenhoof

Getting fired can ruin a day…

…especially when you were the Prince of Hell.

Will Satan survive in English suburbia?

Corporate life can be a soul draining experience, especially when the industry is Hell, and you're Lucifer. It isn't all torture and brimstone, though, for the Prince of Darkness, he's got an unhappy Board of Directors.

The numbers look bad.

They want him out.

Then came the corporate coup.

Banished to mortal earth as Jeremy Clovenhoof, Lucifer is going through a mid-immortality crisis of biblical proportion. Maybe if he just tries to blend in, it won't be so bad.

He's wrong.

If it isn't the murder, cannibalism, and armed robbery of everyday life in Birmingham, it's the fact that his heavy metal band isn't getting the respect it deserves, that's dampening his mood.

And the archangel Michael constantly snooping on him, doesn't help.

If you enjoy clever writing, then you'll adore this satirical tour de force, because a good laugh can make you have sympathy for the devil.

Get it now

Clovenhoof

Oddjobs

Unstoppable horrors from beyond are poised to invade and literally create Hell on Earth.

It's the end of the world as we know it, but someone still needs to do the paperwork.

Morag Murray works for the secret government organisation responsible for making sure the apocalypse goes as smoothly and as quietly as possible.

Trouble is, Morag's got a temper problem and, after angering the wrong alien god, she's been sent to another city where she won't cause so much trouble.

But Morag's got her work cut out for her. She has to deal with a man-eating starfish, solve a supernatural murder and, if she's got time, prevent her own inevitable death.

If you like The Laundry Files, The Chronicles of St Mary's or Men in Black, you'll love the Oddjobs series."If Jodi Taylor wrote a Laundry Files novel set it in Birmingham... A hilarious dose of bleak existential despair. With added tentacles! And bureaucracy!" – Charles Stross, author of The Laundry Files series.

Oddjobs